SNAPSHOTS OF PARADISE AND OTHER STORIES

When Fran first arrives in America she is amazed by the luxurious lifestyle her cousins lead—it feels like paradise! And the most romantic thing of all is Harry, beautiful, bronzed, smelling of water, air and light. But does Harry have any real feelings for Fran or is he just part of the unreality, the dream?

Adèle Geras' short stories take a shrewd look at the differences between dreams and reality, between what we imagine we'd like to be and what we really are . . .

ABOUT THE AUTHOR

Adèle Geras lives in Manchester and has been writing books since 1976. She was born in Jerusalem and much of her childhood was spent in North Borneo, the Gambia and the Middle East.

She used to be a singer and a teacher of French, but is now a full-time writer. Among her novels are 'Voyage', 'Happy Endings', 'The Tower Room' and 'Watching the Roses'.

SNAPSHOTS OF PARADISE AND OTHER STORIES

ADÈLE GERAS

HEINEMANN
NEW WINDMILLS

Heinemann Educational
a division of
Heinemann Educational Books Ltd
Halley Court, Jordan Hill, Oxford OX2 8EJ
OXFORD LONDON EDINBURGH
MADRID PARIS ATHENS BOLOGNA
MELBOURNE SYDNEY AUCKLAND
IBADAN NAIROBI GABORONE HARARE
SINGAPORE TOKYO PORTSMOUTH (NA) KINGSTON

First published in the New Windmill Series 1991

91 92 93 94 95 10 9 8 7 6 5 4 3 2 1

Adèle Geras short stories were first published as follows:

Billy's Hand in *The Methuen Book of Strange Tales, ed. Jean Richardson 1980.*
The Poppycrunch Kid and *The Graveyard Girl* in *Letters of Fire and Other Unsettling Stories* by
Adèle Geras, Hamish Hamilton Children's Books 1984.
The Green Behind the Glass, Love Letters and *Tea in the Wendy House* in *The Green Behind
the Glass* by Adèle Geras, Hamish Hamilton Children's Books 1982.
We'll Meet Again in *Beware! Beware!*, ed Jean Richardson, Hamish Hamilton Children's Books
1987.
Snapshots of Paradise in *Snapshots of Paradise* by Adèle Geras, Atheneum, New York 1983.
The Dreamer of Dreams in *Young Winter's Tales 7*, ed M R Hodgkin, Macmillan 1976.
The Roseline Tape in *Heartache* ed. Miriam Hodgson, Methuen 1990.

British Library Cataloguing in Publication Data
for this title is available from the British Library

ISBN 0 435 12384 X

Cover illustration by Tracey West

Typeset by Cambridge Composing (UK) Ltd
Printed and bound in England by Clays Ltd, St Ives plc

Contents

Snapshots of Paradise

"You some kind of cousin or something, is that right?"
Gene lay on his back on the grass and looked at Fran.

"I suppose I am," she said. "I don't think I know the
proper name for it. My Great-grandmother and
Grandma Sarah were sisters."

"How come she cut and run all the way over there
to England, then? Whyn't she stay here?"

Fran considered. Finally: "She never said. But she
never really became English, you know. Even after
all the years. She still felt she belonged here." Fran
waved her hand to include not only the garden and
the white frame house behind them, but the road and
the apple orchard, the country, the state and the
crazy quilting of all the other states. Coast to coast,
mountain and river, shanty and skyscraper—her
great-grandmother's beloved US of A.

"Betcha nearly took a fit when you heard what
she'd left you in her will," Gene chuckled.

"She wasn't a rich woman," Fran said. "She didn't
leave much. I think an airline ticket is a very good
thing to leave someone."

"You saying you couldn't have made it over here
without her help?"

Being poor was not something Gene could easily
imagine, Fran knew. She felt a desire to punch her
newly-discovered cousin or whatever he was right on
his freckled nose. Spoilt brat! But:

"No, I couldn't," she answered shortly. After all,
she reminded herself, you are a guest in this house.

"Well, you sure picked yourself a fine time," said

7

Gene. "Sixtieth wedding anniversary and all." He nodded at the grown-ups clustering under a huge elm tree. "I don't know why they have to get Ma Jenkins to take the photo. Family group, they call it, like it was something special. I could've done it."

"But then you wouldn't have been in it."

"What about Harry? What're they going to do about him?"

"Patti said they'd bring him down in his wheelchair . . ."

Gene rolled over on the grass, doubled up with laughter. "Hey, that's terrific. That's just about going to kill Harry off, you know what I mean? Can't you just see it? A photograph on someone's table or something for ever and ever, and who's the one in a wheelchair? Grandpa, who's eighty-four? No? Then Grandma Sarah perhaps, who still looks like she could shimmy all night? Maybe Jo, or Patti, or one of the aunts? Maybe Jean, who's always looked half dead? Oh, no sirree, that there's Harry in the wheel-chair . . . Remember him? Track champion? Cheer-leaders' darling? Golden Boy? Superman of 1983 and all the years before that? Isn't that peachy? Just terrific. He's sure gonna love you for that, honey."

"Me?" Fran said, "Why me? I didn't have anything to do with the crash. That happened weeks ago, before I ever got here. Why should he blame me?"

"Won't blame you for the crash, kiddo. Blame you for the snapshot."

"But why? It wasn't even my idea, this family group. I think it was your mother . . ."

"But you're the cousin specially over here visiting all the way from England. Stands to reason you've got to have a shot of the family, right? Besides, it's your camera."

Fran was silent. She glanced towards the house. Sure enough Eleanor, Gene and Harry's mother was

8

pushing a wheelchair across the grass. Harry's hair fell over his brow, shadowing his eyes.

"Why did you call him a Golden Boy?" she asked Gene. "His hair is dark. Almost black. You're more golden than he is."

"Boy, are you dumb!" Gene sat up. "Goldenness doesn't have one single thing to do with hair. Golden, that's the kind of person you are. Successful, handsome, smart. You get what I mean. It's up here." He tapped his skull and laughed. "I'm about as golden as a pair of sneakers with holes in them. Listen to it—you can't hear what they're saying, but I'll tell you: 'Harry, how is it? How's it going, kid? Won't be long before you're back in training . . . Are you too hot? Too cold? Is everything o.k.? Would you like to sit here? Or over there, honey? Is the sun in your eyes? Move that wheelchair a little bit, Eleanor . . .' I could go on and on."

"He's been injured," said Fran. "It's only natural that they should make a fuss over him. I think you're just plain jealous."

"I guess," Gene said. "I guess I am. It's the natural condition for an Ugly Duckling born a brother to the swanniest swan of the lot."

"And look what happened to the Ugly Duckling, Gene," said Fran. "Anyway, you're not one. Not really. Your nose is out of joint, that's all."

"What does that mean? Boy, do I love your English expressions. Person can never tell what you're saying."

"It means—I guess it means you're angry, jealous. I don't know."

"Well," Gene sighed. "I should be used to it by now. I've lived with it for sixteen years. Ain't nothing new to me."

Joe, Gene's grandfather, hurried towards them.

9

From a distance, with his crew-cut hair and military style shirt, he looked like a young man.

"C'mon you kids. Time to get lined up now." Gene and Fran scrambled to their feet and walked over to where the others were in the process of sorting themselves out. Patti, Joe's wife and Gene and Harry's grandmother, seemed to be in charge of organizing the group.

"O.K. now. We've got Grandma Sarah and Grandpa right in the middle. Leave a space behind them for Joe and me, right? Then I guess . . . Yeah, Susan, Rose and Jean, can you kind of group yourselves around Grandma Sarah? Right, that's great. Where's that husband of your's, Rose? Oh! O.K. Bill, I've got you now. Whyn't you come over and still count as one of the younger generation. Come on down here now, near the front, and you kids, right in the bottom row. Let's put Franny between the boys, O.K. Kneel down, that's it. Cross-legged would be even better. Great. We've got it. Now don't move a muscle, anyone. I'll just race round to the back, then you can go ahead and press that button."

Patti tottered across the grass in high-heeled sandals. Ma Jenkins, an unsuspecting neighbour who'd only called in on her way to church to wish the old folks a happy anniversary, came forward hesitantly.

"Lordy, what a responsibility! Is this right? Do I have to focus it? Is this the right button? Gee, I'll feel just terrible if it doesn't come out."

She pressed the button. The photograph slid out of the bottom of the camera. The family group broke up and gathered round Ma Jenkins to watch the ghostly shapes sharpen, to watch the colours brighten.

"Just plain old magic, that's what it is," said Ma Jenkins as she handed the camera back to Fran, relieved that her part in the adventure was over.

10.00 a.m. Family Group

*Grandma Sarah looks pretty in a lace blouse, not much
different from the way she looked back in the 1920s when
she used to Charleston all night in beaded dresses. She has
been married for sixty years to the same man: Grandpa,
who used to be a snappy dresser and now wears a beach
shirt with palm trees printed on it. Patti has on a shirt-
waister dress and wears her hair in bangs. She looks like
an older version of Doris Day. The three weird sisters, (as
Gene has liked to call them ever since he read 'Macbeth' in
High School), don't look like sisters at all. Not to each other
and not to upstanding, military Joe, who is their brother.
Susan is the plump and homely one. She has harlequin
glasses and a big smile. Rose is the skinny, glamorous one,
gold bangles and heavy rings weighing down her hands.
Bill, her husband, is half-hidden behind Joe. That's typical.
Jean looks like an old lady, although she's younger than all
of them. It's the hair in the bun, the brooch at the collar of
the plain white blouse. It's the eyes. Grandma Sarah has
eyes with more youth in them. Eleanor looks like a sister to
her sons. Her long, reddish hair falls over her face. Her
skirt is pink cotton, Mexican, embroidered with flowers and
birds in fire colours. Fran, Gene and Harry are at the front.
Fran is wearing jeans and T-shirt, looking quite American
for a beginner. Gene is looking at her. She is looking at
Harry. And Harry is looking straight at the camera.*

I suppose, Fran had thought when she first saw the
swimming-pool, that this is what they mean by
Culture Shock. A week of being in the United States
still hadn't accustomed her to the idea that ordinary
people (well, quite wealthy, O.K. but not disgust-
ingly, stinkingly rich) had such things right in their
back garden. She spent a lot of time there, partly
because she liked swimming, partly because it was so
hot and partly to talk to Harry. Mostly, perhaps to
talk to Harry. Ever since the crash, he had made a

11

kind of den for himself down by the pool, under an umbrella, with a table next to him, and all the comforts of his room around him, it seemed. Gene had rigged up a portable TV, he had a radio, there were books—anything he could possibly want. Fran felt newly shy each day as she approached him. She felt she was invading his privacy. And today? Would he be angry with her about the photograph? He didn't look angry. He was smiling.

"Hey, Fran," he called as he saw her coming down the steps from the house. "Come on over and talk to me. I'm going crazy in all this heat with no one to talk to . . ."

"Sure," Fran said and sat down beside him. "What do you want to talk about today?"

"I dunno. Life, Love, Art, Death, the usual stuff. You liking it here?"

"It's wonderful. I mean it." Fran laughed. "I never thought it'd be anything like this."

"'Paradise for Kids' my grandmother calls it. Gene and me, we always call it that—I guess it was a kind of paradise when we were kids. But now, we say it kind of sarcastically, know what I mean? I mean the joint round here is not exactly jumping . . ."

"Do you miss the city? Is that it?"

"I guess—my friends, more than anything. And there's nothing to do except talk to your own family. That's why I like talking to you. You're different."

Fran blushed. "Different—is that good or bad?"

"It's good. I like it. I like hearing about England and the stuff you do back there. And I can tell you things. You're family and not family at the same time. D'you know what I mean?"

"May I ask you something then?" Fran said.

"Sure—anything you like."

"Tell me about your father. No one ever mentions him."

12

Harry frowned and said nothing for a moment. Fran looked at him: the smooth brown line of his neck, his straight nose, the toes sticking out of the plaster casts he wore on both legs, and felt as though some part of her, some inner substance of which she was unaware, were dissolving, melting in the warmth of the love she was feeling. She identified it as love at that moment, while she was waiting for Harry to speak. She hadn't thought of it by a name before, only that she liked to look at him, liked the sound his voice made, waited for him to come into a room if he were absent, thought of him, imagined . . .

Now that she had given it a name, Fran felt both anguish and relief. Relief, because it's always a comfort to know the actual name of the disease you're suffering from, and anguish because in five days she would be back in England and Harry would be here, and that would be that. But, said a tiny, hopeful voice from somewhere inside her head, what if he loves you? Really loves you? He could visit . . . You could visit . . . You could marry, have kids. Paradise for kids. Live in Paradise . . .

Another voice, stronger, harder, so much more sensible, also inside her head: "Don't be a bloody fool. Why should he love you? Look at you? Kiss you? Want to marry you, for Heaven's sake? Are you nuts? A face like that? A body like that? A Golden Boy? Forget it."

Fran could picture Harry's future with a certainty that muffled her heart and made her catch her breath: Mr and Mrs Golden, right here in Paradise, a modern equivalent of Grandpa and Grandma Sarah. Almost, she could imagine Harry's sixtieth wedding anniversary . . . Forget it, she thought. Take it out at night, this love and look at it for a while before sleeping. Keep the "what ifs" and the "maybes" for the dark hours. Don't let this love out into the open.

13

"Aren't you listening to me, Fran?" Harry said.

"Of course I am, Harry, go on."

"Well, like I said, he hurt my mom a lot. Just taking off like that without a word to anyone. I was six. Gene was four. I don't like to remember that time. I don't like to talk about it. Later on, there was the divorce and stuff like that, and that was tough, but the worst was at the beginning. Every day I'd get back from school and think: he'll be back today, for sure. Today will be the day. But it never was."

"That's dreadful. I don't know what to say."

"That's O.K. We'll talk about something else. I'll tell you a secret if you like."

"A secret? Great!" Fran smiled.

"But first you've got to turn me over, O.K.? Can you do that, being so little and all?"

"Of course I can. I'm little but tough." Fran wondered how the words came out at all, what with the rush of feeling that seemed to fill her throat.

"Right," said Harry. "You put both arms round my waist and kind of twist and I'll lever myself round with my arms. O.K.?"

Fran nodded. She put both arms around his waist and turned him towards her. His skin was warm from the sun and he smelled. Like what? Air, and water and light and sweat and suntan oil and soap.

"There you go," she said as she pulled him round. She took her hands away as soon as she could and hugged herself to stop the trembling.

"You're not through yet, kid," Harry said. "Slave-driver Harry requires that you oil his back."

"O.K." said Fran as lightly as she could. "Where's the oil?"

"Right there." Fran rubbed oil into Harry's back, moving her hands in long, smooth strokes. She felt drunk: silence filled her ears, a mist of heat seemed to hang over the house, over the pool. Time didn't

14

exist any more. The whole universe had gathered itself up into these movements, this feeling, Harry's skin under her hands. She felt hypnotised, dazed, she couldn't bring her hands to stop and then . . . (How did it happen? Later, she would try and reconstruct the exact series of movements, try to slow them and slow them and play them back in her mind, like a video, frame by frame) . . . There was a hand behind her head and her mouth was suddenly on Harry's and she was breathing him in, tasting him, smelling the suntan oil, and his hair, and then it was over. Fran could think of nothing to say. She looked at the pool, at the house, anywhere but at Harry.

"You're a cute kid, you know that?"

Fran struggled, started to speak and couldn't. She coughed and stood up. In her embarrassment, she put on a false American accent:

"Gee, t'anks!" she said. "I've got to go now. I want to get a picture of the house, from the front. I'll see you later."

"What about the secret?" Harry called after her. "Don't you want to hear it?"

Fran had forgotten all about it, and in view of Harry's behaviour by the pool, didn't much care if she heard it or not. All she wanted to do was to get away by herself somewhere and relive that kiss—the further away the better, but:

"Yes, of course I do. Tell."

"It's Gene." Harry said. "He's nuts about you. Honestly."

"That's rubbish!" Fran laughed. "It can't be true, and even if it were true, he'd never tell you."

"He doesn't have to," said Harry. "I'm his brother, remember? I can read his mind."

Could it be true? Fran felt hot and confused. She had to think. Whatever was she to do now? If Gene loved her, and she loved Harry, and Harry loved—

but who did Harry love? Her? Or was it just a friendly, cousinly kiss? It didn't feel like it. It felt like the real thing, although Fran admitted to herself that she hadn't had enough kisses to be able to spot any differences there might be between them. She shook her head. A person could develop a headache from thinking such thoughts in this heat.

"I'm going to get a shot of the front of the house," she said. "See you, Harry."

"O.K." said Harry, and waved to her as he turned to his book.

11.30 a.m. The House. Long Shot

A large white house set on a grassy slope. Plants grow over the railings of the front porch. There's a row of windows above the porch, and another two windows above that, under the gabled roof. To the right of the house is Grandma Sarah's rose garden. She's been working on it since 1930 and is "just about getting it into shape." She still works on it, when she feels good. Just visible behind the house: a corner of the pool. It looks like a chip of aquamarine lying on green velvet.

Fran was in the kitchen, whipping cream for the strawberry shortcake: Grandpa's favourite and the final touch to a meal that seemed to have been in preparation for days. Susan, Rose and Jean had undertaken to put it together, but it looked to Fran as if Jean were doing most of the work, and the others were just gossiping, to each other and to her.

Susan said: "If Mike had lived it would have been our thirty-fifth wedding anniversary this year," and sighed as she licked a spoon. "Did I tell you how we met? My sisters laugh at me, honey, but I reckon it's the most romantic thing. Mike rang up my boss, see, for something or other one day and I answered the phone, being his secretary. And he didn't say a thing to me, but when he'd finished his business with my boss, he said:

"'Tell that secretary of yours that she's the woman I'm going to marry!'" chorused Rose and Jean, and started laughing.

"Gee, Sue," Rose said "I wish I had a dollar for each time you told that story!"

Jean just shook her head. Susan looked thwarted, sulky, like a small child. She turned to Fran. "Don't pay them no mind, they're just jealous. Nothing that romantic ever happened to them, is all."

Rose smiled slyly, and began arranging plump strawberries on eiderdowns of fluffy cream. "You saying my Bill isn't romantic, Sue? Well, I guess you're right at that. He isn't. But he's steady. There's a lot to be said for reliability. Even predictability. I know where I am with Bill."

Jean, with her back to her sisters, took the empty cream bowl from Fran and winked at her and whispered. "Dullsville . . . that's where she is with Bill. And she knows it, too."

"I hear you whispering there," Sue cried. "Little Jeannie with the light brown hair! What're you whispering about?"

"Fran's telling me all her secrets," said Jean.

"No, I wasn't . . ." Fran began.

"She's kidding," said Rose. "Jean always kids everyone. We reckon that's why she never married. Never did seem to take anyone seriously. Don't let the way she dresses fool you, Fran. Not for a minute. That's just a front . . ."

"Rose! Just because you spend your days all gussied up, doesn't mean that everyone . . ."

"Gussied up, she says. Sue, did you hear that?"

"Cut it out, will you?" Sue, the eldest sister, placed small rosebuds round the cake. It occurred to Fran that she had probably been saying the same to Rose and Jean for half a century. "You're behaving like a couple of kids—bickering . . ."

"Who's bickering?" said Patti, coming into the kitchen. "Why, that is a cake of cakes! Wait till they see that. Seems almost too good to eat. Maybe Fran can take a photograph of it, so that we never forget it. What do you say, Fran?"

"Yes," said Fran, "only I want you, too. All of you. Could you stand behind the cake?"

" Right," said Patti. "Shall I sit right here, behind it?" She smiled as her sisters-in-law gathered around her.

Fran took the photograph.

2.00 p.m. The Kitchen. Patti, Susan, Rose, Jean and the Strawberry Shortcake

On the whorls and lines of the scrubbed pine table, a blue plate holding a skyscraper of a cake: four golden shortcake circles, four snowdrifts of cream, strawberries like spots of blood just visible. Around the base of the cake, pink rose-buds and green leaves. At the other end of the table, Patti sits, and her husband's sisters lean over her shoulders and put their faces near hers so that the eye of the camera can see them all, catch them all, laughing. Happy that the cake has turned out so well. Sixty years married to the same person calls for a cake like this, their eyes say. Patti and Joe will perhaps live to deserve this kind of a cake, but it's too late for Susan and Jean and as for Rose: who can tell?

"What're you wearing tonight, child?" Grandma Sarah, sitting in the rocking chair on the porch looked every inch the pretty old lady Fran had seen rocking on similar porches in a dozen movies.

"My best dress, of course," said Fran, "but you'll be the belle of the ball."

Grandma Sarah laughed. "I always was, you know. Didn't Mary tell you that?"

Fran took a moment to realize that Grandma Sarah was speaking of her own Great-grandmother, now dead. "Yes, she did, of course. And showed me photographs."

Grandma Sarah sighed. "Things would've been quite different now if only . . ."

"If only what?"

"If only I hadn't set my cap at Grandpa. He was Mary's beau, you know. I figure that was why she upped and ran away to England. Poor Mary. I guess it wasn't a kind thing to do, but if you'd seen him in those days . . . Lordy, Lordy, what a man!" Grandma Sarah rocked backwards and forwards and closed her eyes. "Harry has the look of him. I can see him all over again."

Fran tried to make the connection. Harry? Golden Harry and the wrinkled, shrivelled old man in the loud print shirts: the same? Would Harry look like that? Ever? She couldn't believe it.

"You not saying a thing, eh?' Grandma Sarah chuckled. "You've got it bad, I guess. Am I right?"

"I don't know what you mean, Grandma Sarah."

"I mean Harry. You fancy you're in love with him. I don't blame you honey. Only watch yourself."

"You and Grandpa seem O.K." Fran decided not to deny it. "Sixty years together and everything."

"Don't let that fool you, Fran. It's no picnic, being married to a man who's like some kind of candle."

"I don't understand—why a candle?"

"They burn so bright that all the moths around just can't help it they keep coming near and getting burned."

"Moths?" Fran was finding herself more and more confused.

"Other women." Grandma Sarah paused. "They

19

never stop trying to get close. And they succeed, too, sometimes. They get their wings singed in the end, but some of them ... well, they get—they stick around for a while. It's no picnic. Don't let the sixty years baloney blind you to that. It's not been one long bed of roses, no sir."

Fran understood at last. "But it's you he loves," she said. "Isn't it? Here you are together after all those years. Aren't you happy?"

"Sure I'm happy now, child. There's no one going to steal him away now!" She smiled. "But you watch yourself with Harry. He's the same. A candle, if ever I saw one."

Grandma Sarah closed her eyes and before long Fran could tell from her even breathing, she was asleep. The camera was on the table beside her. Fran picked it up and took a shot of her great-grand-mother's sister as she lay in the rocking chair.

3.45 p.m. Close-up. Grandma Sarah

The white back of the rocking chair is like a halo round Grandma Sarah's white hair. The wrinkles are there, and the grey hairs, but so is the delicate nose, and the fine mouth and the soft curves of cheek and brow. And Grandma Sarah is slim. Not as supple as she used to be when she was young, of course not. But much the same shape. Only her feet really betray her. She is wearing slippers over toes that are gnarled and bent like tiny tree roots. Fran saw them once, although they are generally hidden away. Grandma Sarah prefers to remember them as they were: tucked out of sight in satin pumps with diamanté buckles and thin heels. She wears a wedding ring and no other jewellery, although she has plenty, upstairs in her bedroom. She no longer has on the lace blouse she wore for the Family Group. The high neck must have been stifling in this weather. She has changed into cream slacks and a loose cotton top the colour of the wistaria that droops over the roof of the porch and casts a shadow over her hands, clasped unmoving in her lap.

Gene and Fran were riding slowly back to the house.

"I don't know why I agreed to this ride," Fran said. "It's too hot. Why didn't we stay by the pool?"

"I dunno," said Gene, "I like getting out of there sometimes, going off somewhere. It gets to be a bit . . . demanding, especially today. We'd have been sucked in if we'd stuck around. To lay the table or put up the bunting or string fairy lights all over the porch or something."

"Maybe we should have helped . . ." Fran began.

"We'll say we were being considerate, getting out from under their feet . . . It's O.K. Don't worry about it."

"Can we stop for air?" Fran said. "I need a breather. Is there any Coke left?"

"It'll be hot, though," said Gene. "After sitting in the basket for so long."

"That's O.K. I'm used to it," said Fran. "Cokes are always warm in England."

"Is that right?" Gene laughed. "Sounds a real weird place. The more you tell me about it the weirder it sounds."

"The beer is warm too," Fran said.

"You kidding me? Boy, am I glad we got our Independence!"

They sat down by the side of the road in the shade of a tree and drank in silence. Fran lay back on the grass and closed her eyes. When Gene spoke, his voice seemed to come to her from a distance.

"Hey, Fran," he said. "When you go back there, to that weird England of yours . . ." he stopped.

"Yes?"

"Well, will you write back to me?"

21

"Would you write back?"

"Sure I would."

Fran sat up and looked at Gene, who was staring out at the road with his back to her. She said: "You don't look like a letter writer to me."

"Don't think I ever wrote a letter in my life before, but I'd write to you."

Fran smiled. Since Harry had told her of Gene's feelings for her, a lot of the things Gene had said over the days had fallen into a recognisable shape. She had thought he was simply being friendly, but now she understood. What she had difficulty in understanding was her own reaction. She felt—there was only one word for it—powerful. As if she could ask Gene for whatever she wanted and he would give it to her, as though she were a magnet, drawing him. It was quite a pleasant sensation, and she wondered if this was how Harry felt all the time, towards everyone, and how she would behave in his place. Thinking about all this made her feel dizzy: a word from her could hurt Gene. If he knew how she felt about his brother, what would he say? Do? I don't want to hurt him, he's too nice, she thought. He *is* nice. He's not even bad-looking, though he's not Harry, but he's a boy. He's six months younger than me, and small and thin, so he looks even younger. And Harry . . . Harry's a man.

"Yes," she said. "Of course I'll write to you. I'm a very good letter writer, as it happens. You'll keep me up to date with all the family news, O.K.?" (Harry's news—lots of that.)

"You want bulletins about Grandma Sarah's rose garden and Susan's latest diet and you want to know if Jean elopes with the bank manager and runs away to Venezuela, that kind of thing?"

"Just news. You know."

"Right. I guess I could cope with that."

22

"Anyway, I'm not leaving till Thursday. That's four days still."

"Don't remind me."

"Why not?" (Oh, this awful power, making her do it. Making her want to crack open Gene's secret and find his feeling for her, wanting him to tell her . . . Why? What was she going to do if he did say something? Would she tell him about Harry? What? How?)

Gene considered the question. "Because I'll miss you. It's been so great having you here. Showing you things—just doing things together."

Fran felt a sudden wave of affection and tenderness rush over her. She wanted to ruffle his hair and hug him to her as if he were her child.

She said: "I've had fun too, Gene. Really. And of course, I'll miss you." She took his hand and gave it a squeeze.

"Fran . . ." His voice shook. "Do you have a boyfriend or something, in England?"

I should say yes, Fran thought. I should lie. I really should. It would get me out of the situation so neatly. Lie, go on, lie.

"No," said Fran. "There's no one in England."

"Then can I go ahead and kiss you?"

Fran laughed. "I don't know. Are you supposed to ask? Is that how it's done?"

"I guess the usual way is, you fall into my arms and it just kind of happens, like in the movies, without a word being said. But I don't seem to get into those kind of situations. So I've got to ask you, Fran. Do you mind?"

"What? The asking or the kissing?" (Stop, she cried out to herself, stop tormenting him! Look how anxious he looks. Oh, Gene, I don't want to hurt you.)

She put her arm around his shoulder and he turned to her. She closed her eyes. Gene was trembling as he kissed her. She could feel the bones of his shoulders through the hot cotton of his T-shirt, trembling.

Afterwards, he said: "I can't think of a word to say, which is unusual for me."

"We'd better go back now," Fran said. "I bet they will want us to lay the table or something."

They got on to the bicycles and rode along in silence. Then Gene said: "Know what I want to do?"

"What?"

"I want to go back and lock myself in my room and play those few seconds back there over and over again, like some kind of video in my head."

"Why, that's . . ." Fran bit her lip. That's how she felt, she'd been going to say. This morning with Harry. Tonight, she'd sit between Harry and Gene and not know where to put herself. If only I were at home, she thought suddenly, far away from all of them. She'd never realized living in Paradise would have such problems. On the other hand, she reasoned, all the others would be there. I won't be alone with either of them. I'll worry what to do tomorrow. Tonight I'm going to enjoy the party.

"I'll put the bikes away," Gene said as they approached the garage.

"Can I take a photo of you first?" said Fran. "Just standing by the bike?"

"O.K." Gene struck a pose. "Like this?"

"No," said Fran. "Just normal, please."

"You got it," he said and grinned, just as Fran pressed the button.

5 p.m. Close-up. Gene.

His faded blue T-shirt hangs outside his jeans. It is none too clean. Neither are the jeans. There are holes at the knees. On his feet he wears trainers that used once to be white. He has pushed back the silky fringe of light brown hair that usually falls over his face and left a dirty mark on his forehead in the process. But his teeth are white and straight, and the bike is gleaming. Gene may not take great pains with his own appearance, but it's clear he lavishes all the time and attention in the world on anything he cares about.

Fran looked at herself in the mirror and hardly recognised the image that shone back at her.

"Is that me?" she asked Eleanor. "I can't believe it. Thank you so much. You wouldn't think just putting up a few strands of hair and twisting it this way and that could make such a difference. I feel grown-up." She sighed with satisfaction and turned to Eleanor, who bent down and hugged her.

"You look real pretty, Fran. That's a lovely dress too."

"I don't look as pretty as you. I never will."

"Why, that's the nicest thing anyone's said to me for the longest time. I love my boys to bits, but you know, I wish I had a girl sometimes. I really miss not having a daughter."

"And I wish . . ." Fran stopped. She had been about to say: "I wish I had a mother like you, who'd put my hair up in loops and spirals and lend me her pearl necklace for parties," but a sense of guilty loyalty to her own mother prevented her. What would she be doing tonight? Sitting on the old sofa in her rust-coloured cardigan and reading the Sunday papers? Watching television?

"Mom!" came a shout from just outside the door. Harry. "You in there? Can I come in?"

Eleanor looked at Fran, who nodded. Without waiting for permission Harry burst in, pushing his wheelchair across the carpet at high speed.

"Mom, guess who phoned? Ronnie—can you believe it? And she's here. She just got back. Anyway, I asked

25

Patti, and she said O.K. why not, and so I asked her to come over tonight for the party. Isn't that great? Isn't that fantastic?" Without waiting for an answer, he turned the wheelchair round and glided out of the room.

Fran turned back to face the mirror. The image that had pleased her so much only moments before now disgusted her. Harry didn't look at her, didn't even see her. He was taken up with this Ronnie. Who was she? Why had no one mentioned her? And how dare she just turn up like this and muscle in on a family occasion?

"That's wonderful for Harry," Eleanor said. "He and Ronnie are so fond of each other."

"Is she his girlfriend?" Fran forced her voice into a kind of steadiness. Eleanor laughed.

"Harry has girlfriends like other guys have shirts. One for each day of the week. But Ronnie's special to him, I guess. Wait till you see her. You'll see why."

Fran struggled not to cry. If she cried, her mascara would run. If she cried, everyone would know. She felt a moment of pure loathing for pretty, unconcerned Eleanor, who was clever about hair and make-up and so stupid she couldn't see how Fran felt about her son.

"I'd better go down now and help with the table" she said.

"Just wait one second," said Eleanor. "I'm going to take a photo of you right now, just as you are. You look so terrific." She picked up the camera from Fran's bedside table. "Sit where you are, right there on the stool and look up at me. That's it."

Eleanor focused on Fran's face and pressed the button.

"Hey, will you look at that!" she cried. "I'm in the shot as well. In the mirror. Gee, Fran honey, I'm sorry. Why didn't I think of that?"

"It doesn't matter, honestly," Fran said. "Actually, I think it looks interesting like that."

"You're being polite," Eleanor smiled. "I guess that's because you're British."

7.00 p.m. Close-up. Fran, with Eleanor.

The lamp on the dressing-table has edged Fran's hair with gold. Her eyes are shadowed and she is unsmiling. The silky material of her dress falls over her shoulders in folds of scarlet and the pearls round her neck shine from the warmth of her skin. Behind her in the mirror you can see Eleanor, taking the photograph. Her red hair falls over the camera. Her dress is made of chiffon: turquoise, blue, green, mauve blending in an ocean of colour. Also reflected are the wall-lights above Eleanor's head: small, cream lampshades fringed with tassels. A field of soft, pink carpet stretches away to the door.

"I don't think," said Susan, "I'm ever going to eat another morsel as long as I live."

Gene bent towards Fran and whispered: "Five'll get you ten she'll have buckwheat pancakes for breakfast. Wait and see."

Fran giggled. She had been giggling a lot: from the sea-food salad, through the turkey-with-all-the-trimmings, right up to the strawberry shortcake. It must be the wine, she thought vaguely. She looked at Gene, beside her. She looked at Harry and Ronnie sitting right across the table from her. Ronnie. When she'd first met her before dinner, about a hundred years ago, Fran felt the shock of recognition. Ronnie was the female equivalent of Harry. Miss Golden. She and Harry fitted like two halves of a torn dollar bill. Look at the way she dressed! A black and white pinstriped suit, like a Chicago gangster (in June, for goodness sake!) with a black and white checked shirt.

Stripes and checks together—the daring of it took Fran's breath away. Ronnie had straight, blond hair, cut like a boy's, a wide mouth and a skin like all the words in all the make-up advertisements in the world. Fran drank wine, all the wine she was offered to blur the truth which she knew and couldn't bear. This Ronnie, whoever she was, was Something Else. A different league. Almost a different species from herself. She turned to Gene for consolation.

"Isn't Ronnie lovely?" she whispered.

Gene considered. He took a bit of seafood salad and swallowed it. "She's O.K." he said. "If you like the Robert Redford type."

That's when Fran started giggling. Everyone ate too much. There was too much talk. Reminiscences. Fran listened and giggled and looked around. The strawberry shortcake was in ruins: crumbs and blobby bits of cream lay about on the plate, and the rosebuds had long ago fallen off on to the white lace of Grandma Sarah's best tablecloth.

"I think I'm drunk," Fran said to Gene. "I'm seeing things."

"What things?"

"I can't describe it—it's strange." For a moment, or maybe for longer, Fran had felt as if she were a long way away, up on the ceiling, perhaps and looking down on to the table. The people had vanished and only their clothes were left: clothes sitting up in chairs. There was Rose's black lace, leaning over to talk to Joe's tuxedo. Susan's yellow dress billowed over the table. Jean's wine-coloured silk and Patti's beige, Eleanor's sea-coloured chiffon and Grandma Sarah's lavender velvet, draped themselves this way and that. And the arm of Harry's jacket was around the shoulders of a Chicago gangster suit in black and white stripes, right across the table from a red silk dress that was sitting up very straight in its chair.

"Fran honey, where's that magic box of yours?" Grandpa looked down the table at her.

"I'll get it, Grandpa," said Fran. "It's in my bedroom."

"It's O.K." said Gene. "I'll get it. You'll fall over if you try and get up."

"I won't," said Fran weakly, but Gene had gone.

When he returned there was a debate about who should take the picture. Back and forth the talk went, over the crumbs and the patterns in the tablecloth. In the end Fran spoke:

"Listen, Grandpa," she said. "It's my camera and I'm taking this picture. So there." The wine had given her courage. She stood, rather unsteadily at the end of the table and looked at them all. They were smiling.

"Watch the birdie," she said.

10.30 p.m. The Dining Room, Anniversary Dinner.

Everyone is smiling. What does it mean? Grandpa's smile says: I made it. I'm eighty-four and still here and so's Sarah, and these are my children and my grandchildren and great-grandchildren and even a branch of the family tree from England, flown over specially for the occasion, like a florist's delivery. Grandma Sarah's smile is wistful. I'm a good-looking old lady, it says, sure, but for how much longer? She seems to be glancing at Ronnie as if at her own past. Susan's smile is brave—her corset is pinching like hell. Rose's is a little forced. She is smiling at Bill, who smiles obediently back at her. Jean is enigmatic as usual, a Mona Lisa smile. Eleanor grins proudly, and so she should, looking at her sons. Harry smiles at Ronnie. Possessively. She looks happy, happy with herself and with Harry, and with good reason. Gene is smiling straight at the camera. Or, and this is more likely, at the person holding the camera. He is smiling at Fran and his eyes look as if they're pleased with what they're seeing.

29

"It's O.K. Fran, honey. Honest, it's O.K. Really."
Gene was pleading. "You don't have to cry. You don't
have to feel bad about it. It's nothing to be ashamed
of. You just had too much to drink, that's all. I've
cleaned up after people before. At camp and even
right here—why, I clean up after Harry all the time
. . ."

Fran burst into fresh paroxysms of tears. "Don't
tell Harry," she begged. "Please don't tell Harry I
threw up. I couldn't bear it."

Gene looked at her, puzzled. "I won't if you don't
want me to. But it beats me why not. You O.K. now?
Come on into the kitchen and I'll get you a cup of
coffee."

"My head hurts," said Fran.

"Sure it does. Hurt even worse in the morning. You
wait."

"That's terrific. You certainly know how to cheer a
person up."

"I'm just a little ray of sunshine. Didn't you know?
C'mon."

In the kitchen, they drank coffee sitting at the
table. "I still get a kick staying up late, d'you know
that?" Gene said. "I guess it means I'm not an adult
yet."

"I feel as if I could sleep for a week." She paused.
"Gene, I want to tell you something."

"Shoot."

"Back there, it wasn't just the food and the drink,
you know . . . it was something I saw. I shouldn't tell
you really, only I must speak about it. I'm sorry,
Gene. You see, I went out to sit by the pool, just to
get a bit of air and I suppose I was feeling a bit drunk
and then . . ."

"Go on."

"Well," Fran gulped at her coffee. "Harry and
Ronnie were out there. They were . . . well, kissing. I

30

mean, they didn't even see me or hear me they were so taken up with one another. I just fled. I couldn't look."

"That made you throw up? Seriously? You mean because of Harry? You figured I didn't know what you felt about him? You're crazy, Fran. It sticks out a mile. I knew before you did, I guess."

"Didn't it bother you? After—well, I mean, I thought you liked me and everything."

"No percentage being jealous of Harry any more than being jealous of a flower or the Grand Canyon or something like that. Any way, I'm an optimist. I reckoned after you kissed me, I'd quit being a frog and turn into a prince for you, right there on the spot."

Fran laughed. 'This morning you were an Ugly Duckling."

"And you said I'd turn into a swan eventually," Gene stood up and pirouetted round the floor. 'How'm I doing?"

"I like you so much, Gene," Fran said, "you're so nice and funny and kind . . ."

" . . . and handsome and clever. Go on. Don't stop there."

Fran looked down at her empty coffee cup. She said: "I want to explain about Harry. I thought this morning that I loved him, but I can see it now—it wasn't love. It was more like being dazzled . . . It wasn't altogether real. I can't explain it. It was like a picture of love, a dream of it, a sort of fantasy on my part. I mean, this whole place doesn't seem like the real world to me. It's difficult for an American to understand, I know, but for me and for a lot of people who've never been here, the whole place is like a movie we carry round in our heads. Or a hundred different movies: western plains, city streets, beaches full of surfers, Southern plantations. Everything.

31

And Harry's part of that. All tied up with that. Even this house and all of you, even though you're family, seem—I don't know. Remote from my ordinary life. When I'm here, I find it difficult to think about school, and my own little bedroom and the small square of grass that's my garden.

"What about me? Am I a dream, too?" Gene asked quietly.

"No, you're real. You're the only one of the whole lot of them I can picture coming down to the chip shop with me. Riding on the bus to school with me . . ."

"I'll do that!" Gene's face lit up. "Next summer. You wait. I'll be over there, wait and see, and we'll ride all the buses you like and you can feed me warm Cokes. I won't care. I mean it. I'm coming. You expect me. O.K?"

Fran smiled in spite of herself. "How can you be so sure?"

"Well, now, you see. It's a family tradition. Seventeen years old, you get a ticket to Europe. Grandpa practically insists. Only I'm going to skip all that art galleries and cathedrals jazz and just concentrate on England. I can't wait."

"It'll be wonderful if it happens," Fran yawned.

Gene said: "It will. I promise . . ." and then the door opened and Jean came in and grinned at them.

"You kids still up? Do you know what time it is? Look at you. You look a real mess, both of you. Bed. Right now."

"Aw, Jean, c'mon. I don't feel like sleeping—hey, do you realize we have the same name? I feel like I'm talking to myself . . ." Gene laughed and whispered to Fran: "Tomorrow night I'll take you to a drive-in movie." He put his arm around her shoulders and pulled her towards him, whispered in her ear: "You know. We'll kiss so much, we won't see much of

32

what's going on. It's a real Old American Cliché. You'll just love it!"

"Are you kids through fooling around?" Jean said. "I'm supposed to be locking up around here."

Fran giggled and clung to Gene. "Will you take a photo of us, please?" she said.

Jean laughed. "You must be out of your mind, Fran. Have you seen what you look like? Whoever takes photos at two in the morning anyway?"

"Please, Jean, it's very important."

"If it's going to get you guys out of the kitchen, I'll do anything. Go on, then. Smile or something."

Gene and Fran smiled at one another.

2.00 a.m. Close-up. Fran and Gene.

Fran's hair has come down. All the party spirals and curls are hanging round her shoulders. Gene has the sleeves of his evening shirt turned up above the elbows. Also, his tie has disappeared. The shirt is open at the neck. One hand is in Fran's hair, lifting it up a little. Fran looks pale, but she is smiling and so is Gene. No one would know that they'd asked for this picture to be taken. It's as though the photographer didn't exist, as though the camera has caught them off guard just at that moment. Seeing one another properly for the very first time. Knowing.

Tea in the Wendy House

We're very lucky. Everybody says so. Lucky to have parents who didn't throw up their hands in horror and carry on about unmarried mothers, being too young to know our own minds, etc.

"It's very lucky," said my mother, "that you love one another so much. After all, you've known him all your life. He's always been like a brother to you. Not exactly a whirlwind romance."

I said nothing, but my mother didn't seem to notice. She went on: "It's a pity you didn't wait a little longer, but there you are. Look on the bright side. You'll still have your best years left over when your children are grown-up."

"Are they the best years?" I asked. "I thought now was supposed to be the marvellous time, and we're all meant to be living it up, burning the candle at both ends, finding out what we want to do with our lives."

"Yes, well." My mother looked up from the sewing-machine. She was busy giving some final touches to The Dress. "That's true, of course, but I've always thought that youth was wasted on the young. Someone once said that. I can't remember who it was, but I've often thought how true it is. You've got a lot to be happy about. Graham's very good to you, and he's got a job, and of course there's the house. You really have struck gold there. Not so many young people start out with a place of their own. It needs a bit doing to it, I know, but it's yours. You work on it, and it'll be a showpiece in no time."

Showpiece. You wouldn't know just by looking at it. A small, terrace house in a dingy street. No trees. No front garden, just two feet of concrete between the house and the pavement, with a little wall to separate us from the road. No back garden either. A tiny yard full of scrubby tufts of grass trying to look green, and someone's garage wall at the end. Beyond that, more terraces, and windows with grey curtains. It doesn't matter what colour they were to begin with. In this kind of house, in this kind of street, they soon collect a grey film that makes them all look much the same.

Still, my mother was right. We were lucky. Graham, articled to a solicitor well known in the town, with a steady future of respectability clearly written all over his face, had inspired the building society to uncharacteristic flights of generosity. And my parents, who, as Dad put it, "have quite enough to see you right" from the sale of used cars in Dad's showroom, had paid the deposit for us as a wedding present. And I? I had passed my A-levels very nicely, thank you, and perhaps one day, I might be able to make use of them and train to be a teacher when my own child was at school. That was what Mum said, anyway. Meanwhile, we had a house.

"You've no imagination," Graham said the other day, as we stood at the window of what was going to be the baby's room, and looked out at the muddy patch behind our house. "I can fix a trellis to that garage wall, and we can have climbing plants all over it. Next year. And we can plant grass seed. We can have crazy paving, with those stone pots that have flowers poking out of holes. You know, sort of Spanish."

A hacienda in Grafton Road? Perhaps I could wear a mantilla to hang nappies on the line? I didn't say anything, because Graham was so enthusiastic, but I couldn't see it. I was too preoccupied with what I felt:

35

about the baby, about Graham, about *now* to be able to visualize the future. Also, in our house I still think of the woman who used to live there. We saw her once. When we looked at the place for the first time. She seemed very ordinary. But her kitchen wallpaper, from floor to ceiling, was a mad pattern of Dutch tiles, bright blue and white, with little Dutch children in clogs stomping about happily, and cows and windmills and tulips: the works. It made you dizzy to look at it. It wasn't very clean either, so the Delft blue was spotted with grease and damp, brown in some places, yellow in others.

"We'll have to get rid of all this," Graham had whispered then, and I had agreed.

We stripped the kitchen last week, and painted it. Now it's glossy cream and pale blue and beautiful, but I find myself looking out of the window at the broken slats of the fence between our house and the next, and understanding very well why canals and tulips and windmills and clear blue Dutch skies had been important to the woman who stood in that kitchen before me.

The Wendy House is very pretty. The curtains at the tiny windows are spangled with yellow flowers. The wooden walls are painted yellow too, like butter, daffodils and the hearts of daisies. The table is white and there are four little white stools. Inside the Wendy House, everything is comforting and bright. Inside the Wendy House, even on the dullest day, everything is bright and pretty. Yellow and white.

"Let's try it on then," said my mother, and I stood up obediently with my hands above my head while she slid the silky material over my arms. 'There!" she breathed. "I think that's just right now, don't you?" I looked in the mirror. Perhaps not the most beautiful bride in the world, but O.K. I would have been quite happy with something new from a shop, but no, I was to have a Proper Wedding Dress (even if it wasn't white) and a Proper Wedding, with all the trimmings. As my mother put it:

"There's no reason not to have a celebration, just because there's a baby on the way. Perhaps one should celebrate even more." I wasn't going to be cheated out of my Day to Remember, oh no, and neither was she.

This dress reminds me of my first long dress. I was fourteen, Graham was fifteen. There was a dance at the Church Hall. He asked me to go.

"I'm going to that thing on Saturday," he said, leaning against our coal bunker. "You know. At the Church Hall. Want to come?" He sounded as if he couldn't give a damn either way.

"O.K." I yawned, sounding as if I could take it or leave it.

"Seven-thirty, it starts," he said, "and ends at half-past eleven."

"Great." My heart was thumping. I wished he would go away so that I could go upstairs and look at all my clothes. Maybe I could have a new dress. Maybe Mum would make one. We'd walk into that Church Hall, and everyone would gasp. Graham, when he came to pick me up, would stand back and burst into song, like that man in "Gigi": "Why, you've been growing up before my very eyes!"

Mum made the dress. It was red and frilly, and I thought I looked terrific. Graham, when he saw me, looked me up and down and said: "You'll do." And it was wrong. Everyone else was wearing ordinary daytime clothes. They stared at me, but didn't say anything. I wanted to die. Graham, I thought, would hate me, and would never even take me fishing with him again, down on the Canal. Perhaps he wouldn't speak to me again. I danced, and went through all

37

the motions of enjoying myself, but we left early and on the way home I burst into tears, and cried and cried and wouldn't stop. Graham said nothing. That made me furious. I wanted to hit him. We passed the tree stump that we used to play "King of the Castle" on, years ago.

"Lynn," Graham said. "Lynn, come and sit down."

I sat. I was exhausted. I'd stopped crying. I didn't have the strength to squeeze out one more tear. Graham knelt beside me, and took out his handkerchief. Without saying a word he wiped my face gently, holding my head steady with his other hand.

"I'm sorry," I whispered. "I wanted to look just right, and I . . . it was dreadful."

"I thought you looked," he hesitated, "beautiful."

I couldn't see properly in that light, but by the way he kept his head turned away, I could tell he was blushing. I loved him for saying that, for trying to cheer me up. I laughed.

"I looked dreadful," I said. "Well, not dreadful exactly. Just wrong."

"I didn't think so." He sounded angry.

"I'm sorry, Gray. I know you were being kind."

"I was bloody well *not* being kind," he yelled.

"Ssh! You'll wake everyone up."

"I meant it," he whispered. "I mean it." And he bent his head so that his mouth was hidden in the folds of my skirt, and said so softly that I could hardly hear it, but I felt it more than heard it, through the red material, murmured against my leg: "I love you."

I didn't know what to do. Suddenly Graham, whom I'd known all my life, was different. I didn't recognize him. I didn't recognize his voice, the way he was speaking. He looked up. His mouth was trembling. All at once, he got up. I thought: he's sorry now, he's sorry he said all that. He wants to go home. He wants

38

everything to be like it was before. I stood up too. My legs felt shaky. Graham didn't move.

"Are we going home now?" I asked in what I hoped was more or less a normal voice.

"In a minute. Lynn?"

"Yes."

"Can I kiss you?"

I blushed. I could feel the redness spreading all over my face, down my neck, covering me. I didn't know what to say. He took my head between his hands carefully, gently, like someone holding a precious vase. I closed my eyes. He kissed my mouth, and it felt like warm butterflies brushing my lips, softly, quickly, and then it was gone.

We walked in silence. Not touching. When we reached home, we stood for a moment beside the tree near my gate.

"Thank you for a lovely evening," I said. "I enjoyed it."

"Rubbish," said Graham, "you hated every minute of it."

"Not every minute," I said, and then he took my hands and pulled me right up to him. I could feel the warmth of his body. This time when he kissed me, his mouth stayed on mine, and I opened my lips a little, and so did he, and I could taste him in my mouth.

"I reckon," he said, after a while, "that with a bit of practice, we could get quite good at this."

He was grinning. I could hardly walk up to the front door.

"Hey," he whispered after me, "you look smashing."

I went to bed quickly, even though my mother was waiting to hear all the details. I stared into the mirror, expecting to see huge marks like red flowers blazing on my mouth where I had been kissed, but I looked just the same as I always did. Lying in bed, I thought of what Graham had said: 'With a bit of practice." That meant he was going to kiss me again. And then again. And I wanted him to.

That was three and a half years ago. The kisses went on. They changed in character: grew as we grew older. And, of course, after we had become used to them, we wanted more. And different. New excitement. New pleasures. So one thing, as the saying goes, led to another.

Lynn and Mandy are playing in the Wendy House. They are having a tea party. There are teacups made of red plastic on the table, and a little teapot. Lynn and Mandy are Mummies. They have dolls. The dolls are babies. They are pouring pretend tea into the teacups. Drinking it. Pouring more tea. The dolls fall over. They are picked up again.

A boy comes into the Wendy House. He sits on one of the little white stools. He pushes a doll over. Grabs the teapot out of Lynn's hand. Lynn burst into tears.

"Go away! We don't want you!" she shrieks. A lady comes to see what the noise is all about. She understands at once.

"Graham! You mustn't do that. It's Lynn's and Mandy's teaparty. You mustn't spoil it. Go and play on the slide and let the girls get on with their game. They're much smaller than you. You're a big boy of four."

Graham is taken to the slide. He looks longingly at the teapot and the tiny red cups. Lynn and Mandy are passing round pretend cakes. The babies are being naughty. Lynn is shouting at her baby. "Naughty boy! Naughty!"

Inside the Wendy House, everything is bright and pretty.

There's nothing left in my room now. All my clothes are packed in suitcases, stacked in the bedroom of our little house, waiting to be put away. Every single childhood thing that I possess, all the dolls, books, cuddly toys, the posters of David Bowie and John Travolta, everything has been collected by my mother, and put into trunks in the cellar.

"Waste not, want not," she said cryptically. "You must think of your child."

What makes her think that my child will want posters of David Bowie and John Travolta, anyway? They'll be old hat by then. They're already old hat. A child. That's what I still am to my mother. She would never say so, and I probably wouldn't think such a thing if I weren't pregnant, but pregnant-me thinks: she's keeping something of me, something of the child I was, in those trunks down there. so as not to lose me entirely, so as not to lose my childhood completely.

When I first found out that I was pregnant, I tried to run away. I didn't really think at all, not about where I was going, nor about what I would do when I got there. I didn't take any money with me. I didn't pack anything. I just went as I was and got on the first train I could find. To Stoke on Trent. By the time I got there, I'd changed my mind. I phoned Graham at work. I was crying.

"Come and get me, Graham. I want to come home. Please come and get me. I haven't any money."

Graham didn't ask questions. He simply said: "Stay there. Stay in the buffet. I'll be there. I'll come in Dad's car. I'll ring your mother. I'll tell her something, or she'll worry. Wait for me."

"I'm waiting."

I drank three cups of vile, greyish coffee. They seemed to go on and on. Then Graham burst into the buffet, out of breath. He must have run all the way from the car park. He pushed his way through the tables to where I was sitting. He pulled me to my feet, and flung his arms around me and squeezed me as if he wanted to gather me right into himself, never let me go, and we stayed like that for a long time, not

41

speaking, rocking to and fro. The other people all around us must have thought—I don't know what they must have thought.

"Let's get out of here," Graham said at last. "Come and sit in the car."

We walked in silence to where the car was waiting. As we sat down, Graham said: "Please don't ever run away again, Lynn. Do you promise?"

"O.K.," I said. "Don't you want to know why I did?"

"In a minute. I just want to say something first."

"O.K."

"I don't know how to say it. It sounds so bloody corny."

"Go on."

"Will you marry me?"

I started laughing, and the laughter grew and grew, and Graham laughed too.

"I told you it was corny," he said. "But will you? Will you marry me?"

"It looks as if I have to," I said.

"No you don't. But I wish you would."

"Stupid! I do have to. Well, not have to exactly, but I'm pregnant, so it's just as well you asked me."

Graham said nothing. The laughter disappeared quite suddenly, out of the air.

"Don't tell me," I said. "You've changed your mind. I don't blame you. You really don't need to saddle yourself with a wife and baby at nineteen, you know. I can quite see where it would tie you down."

"I'm bloody furious, if you must know," he muttered, with exactly the same look he used to give me years ago if I jogged his elbow while he was making aeroplane models, or walked through his game of marbles, scattering coloured glass balls in all directions.

I screamed at him: "What gives you any right to be furious? You're the bloody father. Whose bright idea was it, anyway? Who wanted me so much that it hurt? Who was it told me all those things? All those LIES? Anyway, who needs you? I'll have this baby on my own, and you can go and get knotted, for all I care!"

He put his head in his hands. "You don't understand, Lynn," he whispered. "You didn't understand. I'm not cross about the baby. I love you."

"You said you were furious."

"I was. I am. But not about what you think. Not about that."

"About what, then?"

"About you running away. Away from me. When you should have been . . . oh, I don't know, running to find me. Do you see?"

"I didn't know if you'd want me."

"That's what makes me angry. That you didn't know that. Do you really think I didn't mean any of those things I said?"

"Well, I thought you did, at the time. But it could have been the white heat of passion, couldn't it? A madness produced by the nearness of my luscious body?"

Graham laughed. "It could, I suppose. But it wasn't. I love you, and I'll tell you something else."

"What's that?"

"I'm quite pleased that you're pregnant."

"I don't know if I am."

"You'll be a lovely mum."

"Is that all? A lovely mum? I used to have ambitions."

"Really?"

"Yes. Trapeze artist, deep sea diver, high powered business woman, inspiring teacher—you name it, I've wanted it. I want to sing at La Scala and dance at Sadlers Wells."

"I don't think anyone can do both, can they?"

"Don't be so damned literal. You know what I mean."

Graham smiled. "Yes, I know what you mean." He started the car.

"We're going home."

"What'll we tell them?"

"The truth."

"Oh Lord. Really?"

"Yes, really. And Lynn? I want you to know something. I asked you to marry me before I knew ... about the baby, I mean. I've always wanted to marry you."

"Have you? Always?"

"Well, since I was about six."

"You never said."

"It just never came up before, that's all."

Lynn and Mandy are having tea in the Wendy House.

"I'm the Mummy," Lynn says, "and you're the little girl."

"I want to be the Daddy." Mandy's mouth puckers up. Maybe she will cry.

"Silly." Lynn is scornful. "Girls can't be Daddies. Boys are Daddies."

"We haven't got a boy."

"I'll get Graham." Lynn runs to the climbing frame. Graham is hanging upside down by his knees from the top bar.

"Graham," she shouts. "Come and play. Come and be a Daddy in the Wendy House.

"Don't want to."

"Come on." She tickles him under the arms and he hits her and climbs down. She pulls him over to the Wendy House.

"I don't want to be a stupid Daddy in a stupid Wendy House."

"I've got cakes," says Lynn.

"Not real cakes."

"You can pretend they're real." She pushes him on to a stool. "You can pour out the tea if you like."

"I'm the baby," says Mandy.

"Can I put her to bed?" Graham askes Lynn.

"Yes." Lynn looks at Mandy. "Bedtime. Lie down over there."

Mandy lies on the floor. Graham covers her with a blanket. "Go to sleep, baby."

Lynn and Graham sit on white stools, sipping pretend tea out of the red plastic cups. The light pours through the sunshiny curtains, and glitters on the glossy, white paint of the table. Inside the Wendy House, everything is bright and pretty.

Lying in my bed, I think: this is the last time I shall sleep here. Every night for the next ten, twenty, forty, sixty years, I shall lie near Graham in the new double bed. My mother has slept in the same bed with my father for twenty-one years and shows no visible signs of distress, or even boredom. Will it be boring, ever? Like a comfy old cardigan that you wear because you're used to it? Perhaps one day I will feel like throwing the old cardigan in the cupboard, and long to wear something wicked: blood red satin or black velvet. Will my daughter (because it will be a daughter) lie in her bed and think of me and Graham as I think about Mum and Dad? Did Mum think the same things about her mother? We are an endless chain of mothers and daughters, all fitting together like a set of Russian dolls stretching to infinity, and it makes me feel dizzy just to think about it.

Yesterday, we finished painting the front room of the house. We painted it white. The curtains were all ready to hang up. Mum had made them. The material, a lovely pattern of small yellow and white flowers, looked familiar to me, although I couldn't place it at first. I knew I wanted it as soon as I sw it.

It stood out from all the other fabrics as if it were lit up.

My mother said: "With curtains like this, you'll think the sun is always shining."

Graham hung the curtains.

"Not bad," he said, lying back on the sofa to admire them.

"I think they're smashing," I said. "I think this whole room is going to look great."

"Come and sit down, Lynn. Come and try the sofa."

"It's no beauty."

"Beggars can't be choosers. We'll save up for a new one. At least it's comfortable."

I sat down and closed my eyes. I felt tired. All the time now I feel tired. It's the baby. Everyone says so. I felt warm, and tired and soft inside, all over.

"I'm very far away," I murmured. "I think someone is kissing me."

"You betcha," Graham whispered. "I'm kissing you. There is some doubt," he kissed my eyes and my lips and my throat and my hair lightly, gently, "that I will ever be able to stop."

"Don't ever stop kissing me. Don't ever, ever stop loving me."

"I never will," he said. "I never will."

"Graham," I said, tried to say, "Graham, we've got so much to do. Do you think we should? I mean, I feel strange here . . . please."

"It's me," he whispered, "remember? It's only me." And he kissed me, and touched me, and held me, and whispered love into my hair and my ears.

Later, Graham went out to get us some fish and chips. I lay on the sofa and looked at the curtains. Where had I seen curtains like this before? I couldn't think, but I felt strangely frightened, and longed for Graham to come back. Why? It was going to be a beautiful room, bright and full of sunshine. It was

46

going to be a lovely life, wasn't it? Wasn't it? I loved Graham. I wanted him. Didn't I? And my baby! I would love her. We would love her. The Dutch tiles had gone from the kitchen and I would sit at the new table and pour tea. I sat up then, just as Graham opened the door.

"Graham," I said, "I've just thought. Where I've seen curtains like that before.

"Well?"

"At our nursery school. Do you remember? We used to have tea in the Wendy House. The Wendy House had curtains a bit the same. Didn't it?"

"Can't remember, really. Here, take this off me."

We ate our fish and chips. Graham talked and talked, and I said very little.

Tomorrow, I'm moving in. Moving into my new home. Into my new life. Into the Wendy House. I should sleep. Beauty sleep. Can't look awful on my wedding day: "The bride wore pale pink silk jersey and purple circles under her eyes." The bride looked haggard--the bride—the girl—the child—Graham's lifelong friend—and life is very long, isn't it? Playmate, companion, partner, till death us do part, or do us part. Which? It doesn't matter, not really. Everything is arranged, all fixed up, painted. Bright and pretty.

There is no one in the Wendy House except Lynn. Mandy isn't there. Graham isn't there. A doll is sitting on one stool. Lynn pours tea into the red plastic cups from the small, red teapot. She picks the doll up and holds it on her lap. The sides of the Wendy House seem higher. Lynn can hear the other children talking, laughing, crying somewhere on the other side of the walls, but she cannot see them. She tries to open the small door, but it won't open. She pushes it and pushes it and the thin wood shakes, but no one comes to let her out. The walls of the Wendy House are covered in a pattern of

47

Dutch tiles: blue windmills unmoving, children in clogs frozen like statues, unbending flowers all in hard blue, and blue and white. Where has the yellow gone? Where are the white and yellow flowers at the window? Lynn rattles at the doorknob. Shouts. No one comes. No one answers her. She can hear them, talking, shouting, not at her. She cannot get out. She goes back and sits on one of the small stools, rocking the doll. The bright blue walls seem to be closing in around her, the ceiling is coming nearer and nearer. She is happy, rocking the doll. She is Mummy. Mummies love to rock dolls. Mummies love to play in the Wendy House. It doesn't matter that she can't get out. She pours another cup of pretend tea. Inside the Wendy House, even on the dullest day, everything is bright and pretty.

We'll Meet Again

"Fan-bloomin'-tastic!" Maddy said, as she peered short-sightedly into a mirror that was, as she put it, "more spots than silver."

She was wearing a brown felt hat and a brown woollen coat, with a fitted waist and a skirt that nearly touched the ground. "This'll be more your size, Celia. You'd better try it on." She took the coat off.

"Wherever did you get all this stuff? It's really amazing. I mean, it looks authentic."

"It is authentic." Celia was pulling the brown coat on.

"Honestly, Maddy, can't you do something about the mirrors? It's difficult to see what you look like. What kind of shop is this anyway?"

"It's not a shop. Hadn't you noticed? Just an oversized box full of second-hand clothes. My customers are used to it. If they want mirrors, they can go to Jaeger or Next or somewhere. Cheapo style, that's what I'm about. These are great, honestly. Forties is all the rage. You said they were authentic. Where did you find them?"

"I was given them. A man in our street let me take them. He was clearing up after his wife died." Celia paused. "She died about two years ago, actually. I think he couldn't bring himself to clear up her stuff, and get rid of it—not for ages. Anyway, when I got there, it was all ready in that box."

"Dead sad, really," said Maddy "when you think of it. Did you know her? The wife?"

"Well," said Celia "by sight, you know. Not to talk

to, not properly. My mum used to go in there and have a chat, now and then. She was fat. Not very pretty. Not when I knew her . . ."

Maddy had stopped listening and gone to lure a couple of helpless-looking people into her clothes-box. Celia stood in front of the mirror and tried to see herself in what little light there was. I look good, she thought. It suits me. Mrs Stockton was skinny like me, back in the Forties. He said so. I wonder how much Maddy'll want for it.

Mr Stockton was standing by the sideboard when I went in. "Just a few things belonging to Irene," he said, and twisted his head round as if he didn't want to look at anything. Not at me and not at the clothes. "They're no good to me now." That's what he said and then he laughed. Not much to Irene either for a long time. She got too big for them in the end.

"There was a time," (he rubbed a clenched fist along the edge of his chin) "when I could have put both my hands in a circle round her waist. She wasn't any thicker than you are now. A slip of a thing, was my Irene." His throat filled up then, like someone with a chesty cough. I think he was having a hard time keeping himself from bursting into tears.

I said quietly: "My friend Maddy'll like these. She's got a kind of stall in Affleck's Palace." He didn't know about the Palace. I told him, "it's where you go in Manchester for good, exciting second-hand stuff. Is it all right?" I asked, "Taking it there . . ." He noddd then.

Yes, Irene was fond of young people, would like to think of them enjoying her clothes. "You should try some," he said, "you're the right size."

"Oh, I couldn't," I said and now here I am in Irene's coat, and he was right. It's beautiful. Anyway, then I couldn't think of anything else to say, so I picked up

50

the box. Looking back, I could see him standing in the window, stroking the back of his hand along his jawline.

"That looks great," said Maddy, when the customers had gone. "You should keep it."

"How much do you want for it?"

"I'll let you have it for nothing. A kind of commission for bringing this treasure to me, and not trying to flog it to anyone else. You can also have a dress—there's got to be something . . ."

She started rummaging about in the cardboard box. "Here you go."

She held out a soft, slippery bit of what looked like nothing very much. "Try that on."

Celia went into the small space behind the bit-of-fabric-on-a-string that served Maddy as a fitting room. This isn't like me, she thought. These aren't my type of clothes at all. Almost as though she had overheard Celia's thoughts, Maddy spoke from behind the curtain.

"I know it's not your type of gear, Celia. Not really, but you should think about it seriously. I mean, that Forties look really does something for you. You can wear that dress to the Forties Night next month."

"What Forties Night?" Celia said, pulling the curtain back.

"Wowee!" Maddy shrieked "you look like a film star from one of those old black and white thingies. What do you mean, 'what Forties Night'? Every few months they have one, down at the Ritz. Everyone dresses up and the music is Glenn Miller and stuff like that. It's great—you must come, Celia. Promise you'll come."

"Not got anyone to come with, have I?" Celia said, pulling the curtain across again. "Still, I like the dress. I'll have that, and thanks a lot."

"Don't mention it," said Maddy. "And you don't

51

need to have a partner. You can come with me and Graham."

Celia muttered something about gooseberries as the dress came up over her head.

"You'll meet someone there," Maddy said. "Do say you'll come. Go on—you've got such a perfect outfit, that dress in this wonderful slippery material with those lovely blue leafy patterns all over it. And the coat on top of course. Please, Celia?"

"Right," said Celia. "I'll come. I'll probably regret it, but I'll come."

"Terrific," said Maddy. "Just for that, I'll let you take your things home in a carrier bag. It's not every customer who gets one of those. I can tell you!"

Later that same day, Celia struggled up the sloping pavement to the station, wishing the books she had to carry to college were lighter. Wishing that Maddy's carrier bag had a decent handle, one that didn't cut your fingers as you held it. She was wearing the brown woollen coat, and had put her own anorak into the bag, but it didn't make it much lighter. She stood on the platform, waiting for the train to Birchwood, watching the dusk wrap itself, mauve and grey and pink, around buildings which suddenly looked soft at the edges. Only October, she thought, and the evenings are coming earlier and earlier.

When the train pulled in, she opened one of the doors, and then stood aside to let a weary-looking woman hung about with folding pushchair, crying baby and assorted bits of shopping, get on before her. As she slammed the door shut, Celia looked out of the window and the train slowly slid away from the station. Someone was standing on the platform, waiting, looking all up and down the line, as if expecting to see someone . . . Celia wasn't looking carefully, only caught a glimpse, and by the time she looked back to see, the figure had shrunk to almost nothing, but it seemed to her that the woman was wearing a brown coat very like hers. She was still peering up and down the platform, up and down . . . Oh well, Celia said to herself, Maddy said Forties styles were in. They're more in than she thought. I'd better find somewhere to sit.

Celia sat down in the first seat she could find. It wasn't a non-smoking compartment, but what the hell, only a ten-minute journey. I'm exhausted, Celia thought. She closed her eyes for a moment, thinking about the silky dress, dazzled for a second by a daydream of herself wearing it under one of those glass balls they had in dance halls, the kind that bounced darts of coloured light around the walls and on to the skin and hair of all the dancers. She opened her eyes.

"Do you mind if I smoke?" said the young man who was now sitting opposite her.

"No . . . not at all," Celia said. Where on earth had he come from? How long, she wondered, have I been sitting here with my eyes closed? She glanced down at her watch . . . only a minute or so. He must have slipped in quietly. He's very polite. Fancy asking if I minded him smoking.

Celia looked at him as he turned his head to look out of the window. Some kind of a soldier, some sort of uniform. Very fair hair. Dyed? thought Celia. You never knew, nowadays. But dark eyes—maybe blue, but dark. A parting in the hair, short at the back and sides and floppy at the front. As the train came into Birchwood, the young soldier stood up and smiled at Celia.

"Cheerio," he said, and turned and walked down the compartment towards the door.

"'Bye," said, Celia, still a little faint from the feelings brought on by that smile. I can't run after him, she thought. I'll use the other door. She jumped on to the platform and looked for him. There he was, already over the bridge and on the other side. I should go after him, she thought. Call out to him . . . being dignified and ladylike doesn't matter anymore—what if I never see him again?

"Stop it!" Celia said aloud to herself and she turned round to make sure she was alone. As she trudged over the bridge to where her father was waiting for her in the car, she told herself over and over again that she had only seen him for a few moments, that she would probably never see him again. And that she was being a fool. Nevertheless, she knew what it felt like to fall in love. It was as unmistakeable as getting a cold, and she recognized within herself all the symptoms: the pain she felt at the very idea of never seeing him again made her want to cry. The headlights of her parents' car broke into a thousand small fragments of light in the tears she hadn't quite managed to blink away.

"I saw you on the train the other day, didn't I?"

"Yes, you asked if you could smoke," Celia said. (Oh, Glory be, here he is again . . . ten whole minutes . . . please, God, let the time go slowly . . . slow it up . . . let him like me . . . thank goodness I'm wearing the brown coat.)

"Well," said the soldier "it's only polite to ask. I should introduce myself. My name's Neville."

"Mine's Celia."

"Delighted to meet you."

(What a funny way he has of talking, Celia thought. None has ever said that to me. *Delighted to meet you* . . .)

"Do you live in Birchwood?"

"I do at the moment, of course," Neville said. "Based there, you know. Training."

54

"Training for what?"

"Army, of course. Lots of chaps training up here, now."

"Oh." Celia was silent, racking her brains. She'd never seen any soldiers around Birchwood, she would certainly have noticed. But then, she'd only lived there a short time. Perhaps it was possible—maybe even a highly secret camp that no one was supposed to know about. Celia was bored by military matters and thought of a way to change the subject.

"Are you meeting someone in Manchester?" she asked.

"Yes, as a matter of fact. It's—well it's a young lady." Neville blushed.

Celia stared at him. She hardly knew anyone who blushed like that. She sighed. That's that, she thought. He's got a girl friend. Wouldn't you know it? First time for six months I meet a decent bloke and someone else has got there first . . .

"Perhaps I'll see you again," he said.

"Yeah," Celia said. "'Bye."

She muttered to herself as she walked towards the barrier: forget him. Forget him . . . he'll never be for you. He loves someone else. As she left the station she looked back towards the platform. Neville still there, waiting. Hope she never shows up, Celia thought. Hope she's run away to Brazil with a second-hand car dealer. Hope she never comes back. I'll take care of Neville.

Celia looked at the lines of rain slanting across the window. Was that the same young woman, still waiting for someone? She was standing on the platform, waiting, but it was hard to see, through all that rain, who it was. The train pulled out of the station.

"It's Celia, isn't it?" A voice interrupted her thoughts.

55

"Hello, Mr Stockton. Fancy seeing you here."

"It's a bit late for you, young lady, isn't it?"

"Not really. I often go home on this train after a film or something. Mum or Dad meet me. We'll give you a lift as well."

"That'll be grand," Mr Stockton sighed. "On a night like this."

Celia said: "Those clothes you gave me . . . I hope you don't mind. I kept a coat and a dress."

Mr Stockton looked at Celia out of dark eyes.

"Mind, child? I'm delighted. Irene would have been delighted. She did think a lot of you. I know that. A properly brought-up child she said, not like some. And I'm glad someone young'll be wearing her things again. You look a little like her . . . she was thin. Had the same colour hair too. Fine, like a baby's it was, that soft. Eeh, I wish I had a pound for every time I've been up and down to Manchester on this line. I did my training up at Birchwood during the war, like many others, you know. Oh yes. And back and forwards I used to go, to meet Irene in Manchester."

"Did you go dancing?"

Mr Stockton chuckled. "Yes, dancing, and to the cinema and did a bit of spooning too . . ." he sighed. "Same as you get up to with your young man, I've no doubt."

"I haven't got a young man," Celia said.

"You will have," Mr Stockton said. "There's no rush." Celia opened her mouth to tell him about Neville, then changed her mind. She said nothing.

"Nearly home now," said Mr Stockton. "There was a time when it was all aircraft noises round here. In the War."

"You look—different tonight," said Neville. "I mean you look very smart, of course, and you remind me . . ."

"Yes?" Celia asked.

"Well, you remind me of someone."

"Is it your friend? The young lady you're always going to meet?" Celia was all dressed up for Forties Night at the Ritz in the silky dress and the brown woollen coat.

"Yes—yes you look very much like her. Especially now. Have I told you that before?"

"Once or twice."

Neville looked away. "I'm sorry. You see, it's not that I don't like you. I like you most awfully—I mean I *could* like you, but I have promised her . . ."

"But you say she's never there. Never at the station where she said she was going to be." Celia's voice was full of anger. "I hate to say this, but I think she's gone off you. I do really. Otherwise, why doesn't she turn up, eh? Honestly, Neville, face the facts. Please."

The train was slowing down. The lights of the platform slipped past the window like bright beads. Celia stood up and Neville followed her.

"Celia!" Neville put out a hand, touched her sleeve.

"Yes?"

"You don't understand. I *have* to meet her—she's waiting for me, it's just that I have to find her . . . You can't possibly understand."

"Don't talk about understanding," Celia shouted. "I'm fed up with it. Damn it, where's all your fine understanding? Can't you see that I love you? What do I have to do? Walk around with a sign on?"

Neville took Celia's face in his hands and kissed her softly on the mouth, so softly that she hardly felt it, and yet a shiver ran through her as if his lips had been ice-cold.

"I didn't know," he said. "I'm sorry. But I have to wait for her. I didn't know."

The train stopped. Celia tore the door open, jumped

57

out and ran towards the barrier. Through a fog of tears she could see Maddy.

"What's the rush?" Maddy said. "You look as if you're running to save your life."

"It's Neville. I'm fed up with him."

"Ah, the mysterious unknown soldier. Let's get a squint at him. Where is he?"

"Up there, probably. That's where he usually is. Hanging about. Waiting for her."

"Can't see a thing. Not a handsome soldier in sight anywhere. Come on, chuck, let's go and rustle up some grub, and then hit the Ritz with everything we've got." Maddy shimmied down the hill towards Oxford Road singing, asking innocent passers-by whether this was, indeed, the Chattanooga Choo-Choo. Celia followed her, stiff with misery.

"It isn't that bad, is it?" asked Maddy.

"It's terrible. All those people sweating and everybody looking so—so—"

"So what?"

Celia sighed. "So *fleshy*. So . . ." She could find no words.

Maddy put an arm around her shoulders. "You don't mean any of that. You mean, they weren't this Neville of yours."

"He's not 'of mine'," Celia said. "He's someone else's. I'm sorry, Maddy, I'm going home. You and Graham stay. I'll be O.K. Station's only across the road. Can you phone my mum and tell her I'm on the 11.18? I don't feel like talking to her—and I can't stand the music, Maddy, and that's the truth."

"What's the matter with it? It's great."

"It makes me feel like crying. All that stuff about not knowing where and not knowing when, and the blue skies driving dark clouds far away. I've never really thought before what it must have been like"—

58

she paused—"to be in love with someone who could die at any moment, and to be in danger yourself."

"Go home," said Maddy. "I can see what kind of mood you're in. And Graham's walking you up the hill, and I don't care what you say."

"I'll go and get my coat," Celia said.

Celia huddled against one of the pillars, trying not to be seen. The clock on the platform said 11.15. Three more minutes ... Oh, please, *please*, she thought, make him not look up. Make him not see me. She bit her lip and felt hope, any hope she had at all, drain out of every bit of her. Across on the other platform she could see them quite clearly, standing under one of the lights. They stood close together. He had found her at last, his girl, the one he had been coming to meet all those other times.

He was looking down at her. She seemed to fit herself into the circle of his arms, khaki against the brown fabric of her coat. A coat a lot like this, Celia thought, and glanced at them again. They had turned to leave now. Neville still had his arm around the woman. It seemed to Celia that his arm was fixed there forever, that nothing could move it. At the barrier they stopped and the woman stood on tiptoe so that he could kiss her. Celia watched them and felt sick. Where the hell was the train? She began to cry as it came into the station.

"Lovey," said Celia's mother, "what is it? What's happened? You surely can't have heard ..."

"No, I'm fine ... really. I just—it doesn't matter. Heard what?"

"About poor old Mr Stockton."

"What about him?"

"He died. Just about half an hour ago, that's all."

"How do you know?"

"Betty told me. She heard a crash. He'd pulled an armchair over as he fell. It was very quick. He can't have felt any pain. Poor thing . . . I feel sad. He hasn't any children or close family that we know of. I'll have to go over there and help Betty pack up his stuff. Tomorrow probably, or the next day. D'you want to give me a hand, love?"

"Might as well," said Celia. I don't think I'll ever care strongly about anything ever again, she thought. My whole body feels like a mouth does after an injection at the dentist's. Numb, but with layers of pain hidden away, hidden deep down and far away. The darkness makes you still, Celia thought the next day. She and her mother and Betty, Mr Stockton's next door neighbour, were packing the old man's life away in cardboard boxes. Yesterday he was here, and now he isn't, she said to herself. Yesterday, when Neville kissed me in the corridor of the train, I thought there was a chance, a hope of something, and now I know there isn't. I should be able to pack the remains of what I feel into a box and give it to Oxfam. Get rid of it.

"How are you getting on?" Celia's mother shouted from the kitchen.

"Fine," Celia yelled back. "Just doing these albums . . ."

"Having a peep, are you?" Celia's mother came into the room.

"Can't help it. I'm nosey and I love all these old brown photos. Only some of them are so small, you can hardly see what anybody looks like."

"There's one fallen out, Celia. Be careful."

Celia's mother bent to pick up the photograph. She smiled. "This is a bit more like it. A bit bigger. Goodness, look at Irene Stockton on her wedding day! During the War, it must have been—he's in uniform. Registry Office wedding, of course. Look how thin

60

and pretty she was, and as for him, well, you'd never believe it was the same person as our Mr Stockton. Here, take it and push it in somewhere. I've got to get back to the kitchen . . ." Celia's mother left the room.

Celia sat looking at the photograph for a long time, and allowed herself to cry. Not for Mr Stockton, who had found his Irene at last, pretty in her silky, leaf-strewn dress and brown woollen coat. Nor for Neville, the young soldier Mr Stockton used to be, whose face smiled up at her now from the wedding photograph. But for her own mixture of regret and happiness: regret because she knew that she would never see him again, and happiness in discovering that love was indeed, as she had always suspected, stronger than death.

The Green Behind the Glass

The telegram was addressed to Enid. Sarah put it carefully on the table in the hall. The white envelope turned red in the light that fell through the coloured squares of glass above the front door. She had no desire to open it. She knew that Philip was dead. The possibility that he might be wounded, missing, captured, never occurred to her. It was death she had been expecting, after all. These were only the official words setting it out in writing. For a moment, Sarah wondered about the people whose work it was every day to compose such messages. Perhaps they grew used to it. The telegraph boy, though, couldn't meet her eyes.

"Telegram for Miss Enid Hurst," he'd said.

"I'll take it. I'm her sister. They're all out."

"Much obliged, I'm sure." He had thrust the envelope into her hand and run towards the gate without looking back, his boots clattering on the pavement. The envelope had fluttered suddenly in a rush of wind.

Sarah sat on the oak settle in the hall and wondered whether to take the message to Enid in the shop. To them, she thought, to the writers of this telegram, Philip is Enid's young man. He was. Was. Haven't we been embroidering and stitching and preparing for the wedding since before the War? Enid will enjoy mourning, thought Sarah. It will become her. She will look elegant in black, and she'll cry delicately so as not to mar the whiteness of her skin,

62

and dab her nose with a lace-edged handkerchief, and wear Mother's jet brooch, and all the customers will sigh and say how sad it is, and young men will want to comfort and console her, and they will, oh yes, because she didn't really love him.

"She didn't really love him," Sarah shouted aloud in the empty house, and blushed as if there were a part of Enid lurking somewhere that could overhear her. "Not really," she whispered. "Not like I did." I know, she thought, because she told me.

Enid is sewing. I ask her: "Do you really love him, Enid? Does your heart beat so loudly sometimes that you feel the whole world can hear it? Can you bear it, the thought of him going away? Do you see him in your dreams?"

"Silly goose, you're just a child." She smiles at me. She is grown-up. Her face is calm. Pale. "And you've been reading too many novels. I respect him. I admire him. I am very fond of him. He is a steady young man. And besides, ladies in real life don't feel those things, you know. It wouldn't be right."

But I felt them, thought Sarah. And other feelings, too, which made me blush. I turned away, I remember, so that Enid should not see my face, and thought of his arms holding me, and his hands in my hair and his mouth . . . oh, such a melting, a melting in my stomach. I loved him. I can never say anything. I shall only be able to weep for him at night, after Enid has fallen asleep. And I shall have to look at that photograph that isn't him at all, just a soldier in uniform, sepia, like all the soldiers. Enid will keep it there between our beds. Perhaps she will put it in a black frame, but after a while, I shall be the only one who really sees it.

Sarah tried to cry and no tears would come. It seemed to her that her heart had been crushed in metal hands, icy cold and shining. How could she bear the tight pain of those hands? But soon, yes, she would have to take the telegram and walk to the shop and watch Enid fainting and Mother rustling out from behind the counter. Mrs Feathers would be there. She was always there, and she would tell, as she had told so often before, the remarkable story of her Jimmy, who'd been posted as dead last December, and who, six months later, had simply walked into the house, bold as you please, and asked for a cup of tea.

"You're mine now," Sarah said aloud to the telegram, and giggled. Maybe I'm going mad, she thought. Isn't talking to yourself the first sign? I don't care. I don't care if I am mad. I shall go and change into my blue dress, just for a little while. Later, I shall have to wear dark colours, Philip, even though I promised you I wouldn't. Mother will make me wear them. What will the neighbours say, otherwise?

"Philip is like a son to me," Mother used to say, long before he proposed to Enid. "One of the family." Perhaps that is why he proposed. Or perhaps Mother arranged the whole thing. She is so good at arranging. Enid is piqued, sometimes, by the attention Philip pays to me. I am scarcely more than a child. Mother says: "But of course, he loves Sarah, too. Isn't she like a little sister to him?" When she says this, I clench my fists until the nails cut into my palms. I don't want that kind of love, no, not that kind at all.

Sarah laid the blue dress on the bed, and began to take off her pinafore. The sun shone steadily outside, but the leaves had gone. Swiftly, she pulled the hat box from under the bed, and lifted out her straw hat with the red satin ribbons. It was a hat for long days of blue sky, green trees and roses. I can't wear it in November, she thought. It had been wrapped in tissue paper, like a treasure. Sarah had looked at it often, remembering the afternoon in Kew Gardens,

64

so long ago, a whole three months. She had thought of it as the happiest day of her life, a day with only a small shadow upon it, an insignificant wisp of fear, nothing to disturb the joy. But now Philip was dead, and that short lived moment of terror spread through her beautiful memories like ink stirred into clear water.

Enid's sewing basket was on the chest of drawers. Sarah was seized suddenly with rage at Philip for dying, for leaving her behind in the world. She took the dress-making scissors out of the basket, and cut and cut into the brim of the hat until it hung in strips, like a fringe. The ribbons she laid beside her on the bed and she crushed the crown in her hands until the sharp pieces of broken straw pricked her, hurt her. Then she snipped the long, long strips of satin into tiny squares. They glittered on her counterpane like drops of blood. When she had finished, her whole body throbbed, ached, was raw, as if she had been cutting up small pieces of herself. She lay back on the bed, breathless. I must go to the shop, she told herself. In a little while. If I close my eyes, I can see him. I can hear his voice. And Enid's voice. Her voice was so bossy, that day:

"You can't wear that hat," Enid says. "It's too grown up."

'I am grown-up.' I dance round the kitchen table, twirling the hat on my hand, so that the ribbons fly out behind it. "I shall be seventeen at Christmas, and it's just the hat for Kew."

"I don't know why you're coming, anyway," says Enid.

"She's coming because it's a lovely day, and because I invited her," Philip says.

He is leaning against the door, smiling at me.

"Thank you, kind sir." I sweep him a curtsey.

"A pleasure, fair lady," he answers, and bows gracefully.

"When will you two stop clowning?" Enid is vexed. "You spoil her all the time. I've had my hat on for fully five minutes."

"Then let us go," he says, and offers an arm to Enid and an arm to me.

In the street, Enid frowns: "It's not proper. Walking along arm in arm . . . like costermongers."

"Stuff and nonsense," says Philip. "It's very jolly. Why else do you suppose we have two arms?" I laugh. Enid wrinkles her nose.

"August is a silly time to come here." There is complaint in Enid's voice. She is sitting on a bench between me and Philip. "The camellias are long since over, and I love them so much. Even the roses are past their best." She shudders. "I do dislike them when all the petals turn brown and flap about in that untidy way."

"Let's go into the Glass House." I jump up and stand in front of them. Enid pretends to droop.

"Philip," she sighs, "you take her. I don't think I could bear to stand in that stifling place ever again, among the drips and smells."

Philip rises reluctantly, touches Enid's shoulder.

"What about you, though?" he says. "What will you do?"

"I shall sit here until you return." Enid spreads her skirts a little. "I shall look at all the ladies and enjoy the sunshine."

"We'll be back soon," I say, trying to keep my voice from betraying my excitement. Have I ever before been alone with him? Will I ever be alone with him again? Please, please, please, I say to myself, let the time be slow, don't let it go too quickly.

Phlip and I walk in silence. I am afraid to talk, afraid to open my mouth in case all the dammed-up love words that I am feeling flood out of it.

We stand outside the Glass House for a moment, looking in at the dense green leaves pressing against the panes. A cloud passes over the sun, darkens the sky, and we are both reflected in the green. Philip's face and mine, together. In the dark mirror we turn towards each

66

other. I stare at his reflection, because I dare not look at him, and for an instant his face disappears, and the image is of a death's head grinning at me, a white skull: bones with no flesh, black sockets with no eyes. I can feel myself trembling. Quickly, I look at the real Philip. He is there. His skin is brown. He is alive.

"What is it, Sarah? Why are you shaking?"

I try to laugh, and a squeak comes from my lips. How to explain? "I saw something reflected in the glass," I say.

"There's only you and me."

"It was you and me, but you . . . you had turned into a skeleton."

The sun is shining again. Philip's face is sad, shadows are in his eyes as he turns to look. I look too, and the skull has vanished. I let out a breath of relief.

"It's only me, after all," he says.

"But it *was* there. I saw it so clearly. Philip, please don't die."

"I shan't," he says seriously, carefully. "I shan't die. Don't be frightened. It was only a trick of the light."

I believe him because I want to believe him. He takes my hand. "Let's go in," he says.

Inside the Glass House, heat surrounds us like wet felt. Thickly about our heads a velvety, glossy, spiky, tangled jungle sucks moisture from the air. Leaves, fronds, ferns and creepers glisten, wet and hot, and the earth that covers their roots is black, warm. Drops of water trickle down the panes of glass. The smell of growing is everywhere, filling our nostrils with a kind of mist. We walk between the towering plants. There is no one else there at all. A long staircase, wrought-iron painted white, spirals upwards, hides itself in green as it winds into the glass roof. Philip is still holding my hand, and I say nothing. I want him to hold it forever. I want his hand to grow into mine. Why doesn't he speak to me? We always laugh and joke and talk so much that Enid hushes us perpetually, and now he has nothing to say. I think: perhaps he is angry. He wants to sit with Enid in the cool air. He is cross at having to come here when his time with Enid is so short. He is leaving tomorrow, and I have parted them with my selfishness and my love. Tears cloud my eyes. I stumble, nearly falling. My hat drops to the ground. Philip's hand catches me round the waist. I clutch at his arm, and he holds me, and does not let me go when I am upright. We stand, locked together. "Sarah ..." It is a whisper. "Sarah, I must speak." The hand about my waist pulls me closer. I can feel the fingers spread out now, stroking me. Philip looks away. "I can't marry Enid," he says. "It wouldn't be right."

"Why?" There are other words, but they will not come.

"I can't tell her," he mutters. "I've tried. I can't." He looks at me. "I shall write to her. Soon. It's a cowardly thing to do, but I cannot bear to face her ... not yet. Not now. Sarah?"

"Yes?" I force myself to look up.

"Sarah, do you know," his voice fades, disappears, "... my feelings? For you?"

"Me?" My heart is choking me, beating in my throat.

"I ... I don't know how to say it." He looks over my head, cannot meet my eyes. He says, roughly: "I've thought it and thought it, and I don't know how to say it." He draws me closer, close to him. I can feel his buttons through my dress. I am going to faint. I am dissolving in the heat, turning into water. His arms are around me, enfolding me. His mouth is on my hair, moving in my hair. Blindly, like a plant in search of light, I turn my face up, and his lips are there, on my lips, and my senses and my nerve ends and my heart and my body, every part of me, all my love, everything is drawn into the sweetness of his mouth.

Later, we stand together, dazed, quivering. I can feel his kiss still, pouring through me.

"Philip, Philip," I bury my head in his jacket. "I love you. I've always loved you." Half hoping he will not hear me. He lifts my face in his fingers.

"And I love you, Sarah. Lovely Sarah, I love you. I don't know how I never said it before. How did I make such a mistake?"

68

I laugh. Everything is golden now. What has happened, what will happen, Enid, the rest of the world, nothing is important.

"I'm only a child," I say smiling, teasing.

"Oh no," he says, "no longer. Not a child." He kisses me again, softly. His fingers are in my hair, on my neck, touching and touching me. I have imagined it a thousand times and it was not like this. Wildly, I think of us growing here in this hothouse forever, like two plants curled and twined into one another, stems interlocked, leaves brushing . . . I move away from him.

"We must go back," I say.

"Yes." He takes my hat from the ground and puts it on my head.

"You must promise me," he says, "never to wear mourning."

"Mourning?" What has mourning to do with such happiness?

"If I die . . ."

"You won't die, Philip." I am myself again now. "You said you wouldn't. I love you too much. You'll come back, and we'll love one another forever, and live happily ever after, just like a prince and princess in a fairy tale."

He laughs. "Yes, yes we will. We will be happy."

Walking back together to Enid's bench, we make plans. He will write to me. He will send the letters to Emily, my friend. I shall tell her everything. He will write to Enid. Not at once but quite soon. We can see Enid now. She is waving at us. We wave back.

"Remember that I love you," Philip whispers when we are nearly oh, nearly there. I cannot answer. Enid is too close. I sit on the bench beside her, dizzy with loving him.

"You've been away for ages," she says. "I was quite worried." His voice is light, full of laughter. "There's such a lot to look at. A splendid place. You really should have come."

I am amazed at him. I dare not open my mouth. Here in the fresh air, I cannot look at Enid. The dreadfulness of what I am doing to her, what I am going to do to her makes me feel ill. But how can I live with my love pushed down inside me forever? Will she forgive us? Will we have to elope? Emigrate? There will be time enough to worry when she finds out, when Philip tells her. Now, my happiness curls through me like a vine. We set off again along the gravel paths. I have to stop myself from skipping. I remember, briefly, the skeleton I saw reflected in the glass, and I laugh out loud at my childish fear. It was only a trick of the light, just as Philip had said. A trick of the light.

There are stone urns near the Temperate House, and curved stone flowers set about their bases. A lady is sitting on a bench in the sunshine under a black silk parasol. The light makes jagged pools of colour in the inky taffeta of her skirts and her hat is massed with ostrich feathers like funeral plumes. She turns to look at us as we go by, and I see that her face is old: small pink lips lost in a network of wrinkles, eyes still blue, still young under a pale, lined brow. She wears black gloves to cover her hands and I imagine them veined and stiff under the fabric. She smiles at me and I feel a sudden shock, a tremor of fear.

Enid says: "Forty years out of date at least. Do you think she realises how out of place she looks?"

"Poor old thing," says Philip. "Rather like a pressed flower, all alone in the world." He whistles the tune 'Mademoiselle from Armentières.' "How would you like it?"

"I hope," says Enid, "that if I ever wear mourning, I shall not be so showy. Ostrich feathers, indeed! Mutton dressed as lamb."

I look back at the old woman, marvelling at Enid and Philip for finding her interesting enough to talk about. I feel pity for her, and a faint amusement, but she does not hold my attention. She is as remote from me, as strange, as if she belonged to another time. I start to run across the grass, as fast as I can. They are chasing me, yes, even Enid, dignity forgotten, is running and running. We stop under a tree, all of us breathless.

Philip puts his hands on my waist and twirls me round. I glance fearfully at Enid, but she is smiling at us like an indulgent mother.

We walk home in the dusk. I must leave him alone with Enid at the gate. He kisses me goodbye on the cheek, like a brother, and I go indoors quickly. I am burning in the places where he touched me.

Sarah sat up. Slowly, like a sleepwalker, she gathered up the torn, bruised straw and the scraps of ribbon from the bed and the floor, and put them in the hatbox. When there is time, she thought, I shall burn them in the kitchen fire. She struggled into the blue dress and looked at herself in the mirror. What she saw was the face of a stranger who resembled her: mouth pulled out of shape, skin white, hair without colour. She fastened, carefully, the buttons on her cuffs. Her skin, all the soft surfaces of her body, felt raw, scraped, wounded. I am wounded all over, she thought, and went slowly downstairs. She put the telegram in her pocket, and left the house.

1917 May

"I think James will come to call this afternoon." Enid's fingers make pleats in the lilac skirts she was wearing.

Sarah said: "Do you like him?"

Enid considered the question. The sisters were walking in Kew Gardens. Enid wanted to see the camellias. "Yes," she said at last, "he is a fine man." Sarah thought of James's solid body and long teeth, his black hair and the small brush of his moustache. Over the months, scars had slowly covered the sore places in her mind but sometimes, especially at Kew, the pain took her breath away. She should not, she knew, walk there so often, but she did. She should have avoided the Glass House, but she went there at every opportunity, and stood beside the streaming

71

panes with her eyes closed, willing herself to capture something. Her feelings on that day had been so overpowering, had filled her with such sharp pleasure that always she hoped that their ghosts must still be lingering among the leaves.

Now, she looked at Enid. "I think," she said, "that he will suit you very well."

"He hasn't proposed to me yet," Enid said placidly. "Although I don't think it will be too long. In any case, I shall have to wait at least until November . . ." Her voice trailed away, losing itself among the branches.

"Philip," Sarah said (and the word felt strange in her mouth, an unfamiliar taste, like forgotten fruit), "Philip would be pleased to think you were happy."

"Do you think so, really?" Enid looked relieved. "Of course, I was heartbroken, heartbroken at his death. You remember? I fainted, there and then on the floor of the shop I shall never forget it."

"Neither shall I," said Sarah.

Enid comes out from behind the counter. She says: "What's the matter, Sarah? Are you ill? You look so white. Why are you wearing that thin dress?"

Mother is talking to Mrs Feathers. It is absorbing talk. I do not think they have seen me.

I say nothing. I give the envelope to Enid. She tears it open: a ragged tumbling of her hands, not like her at all.

"It's Philip," she says. "Philip is dead."

I watch, mesmerized, as she falls in a liquid movement to the ground.

Mother loosens Enid's collar, her waistband, brings out smelling salts. She is weeping noisily. Mrs Feather says: "I'll put the kettle on for a cup of tea. Plenty of sugar, that's the thing for shock."

I envy my mother every tear she is shedding. I want to cry, and I cannot. The iron grip tightens round my heart.

"His letters," said Enid, "in the months before his death were quite different, you know. Did I ever tell you?"

"No."

"More formal. Veiled. Forever talking about an important matter which we would discuss on his next leave. Not so . . . devoted."

Sarah tried to stop herself from feeling happy at this revelation.

"His last letter was particularly strange," Enid went on. "He was going to tell me something, he said. He couldn't bear to wait another day, but then the letter finished in a scrawl, messy and rushed, because, I suppose, they had to go and capture some hill or bit of wood. I shall never know what it was."

"It doesn't matter now," said Sarah.

"It is vexing, however," Enid said. "I should have liked to know." Part of Sarah longed to tell her, to tell her everything. But she said nothing. They walked on, in the direction of the Temperate House.

"Look," said Sarah. "She's there again. The old lady."

"She looks," said Enid, "as though she hasn't moved since last August. I do believe that is the same dress."

"And the same hat," Sarah added. "Perhaps it's a favourite. It is certainly smart, even though it's black."

"Come this way, Sarah. I don't want to walk past her."

"I do. I want to."

"Then I shall wait for you over there. Truly, I don't understand you sometimes."

I don't understand myself, Sarah thought. Why am I doing this? She began to follow the same path that they had taken before. Almost she could hear Philip whistling . . . Mademoiselle from Armentières . . . hasn't been kissed for forty years . . . hasn't been

73

kissed . . . The air seemed colder. Sarah turned her head away a little as she passed the bench. The lady said: "Such a lovely day, my dear. Don't you think it's a lovely day?"

Under the black feathers, the lady smiled at her, and Sarah could see in her eyes long memories of past happiness, past youth, past love.

"Yes," she said. "Lovely."

"I've seen you here before," the lady said.

"I come quite often. I like it here."

"You had a hat with red ribbons, I remember. I remember many things, and I recall that hat, because I had one once, too, and when I saw you . . ." The lady looked down.

"Yes?"

"You will think it absurd. But there, at my age, I'm permitted to be a little foolish. I thought I was seeing a ghost. A ghost of myself, when I was young."

Sarah smiled, a little nervously. "I must go back to my sister now," she said. "I think your hat is lovely."

The lady smiled, nodded, did not answer.

Sarah walked back to where Enid was waiting. She glanced towards the Temperate House, but the old lady had gone. There was no sign of her anywhere.

Later, on their way home, Sarah and Enid passed by the Glass House. "Are you going in today?" Enid asked.

"No," said Sarah. "I'm only looking in."

She stared at her reflection in the pane dark with the darkness of the green behind it, and touched the veiling that trimmed her hat. At first she did not recognize herself. The veiling looked . . . could it be . . . like feathers? Surely her mouth was not so shrunken, nor her cheeks so white? Her hands seemed stiff, she looked old, she looked wrinkled, she looked—no, no, she couldn't, wouldn't look, like the faded old lady on the bench. A pressed flower, Philip had said. She shook her head, moved it closer to the glass, and the image changed. She was herself again. There was her hat, her own face, still young. She shivered. A trick of the light, that was all it was. Only a trick of the light.

"I don't think," she said to Enid as they walked through the tall wrought-iron gates, "I don't think I shall be coming to Kew ever again."

Love Letters

I

"Dearest Pete" or "Pete, dearest" or "Pete, my dearest" or "Pete, my darling" or just "Darling Pete"—which to choose? It was, after all, the first letter and didn't things like how you addressed him have to climb a kind of ladder? Marion decided finally that she'd start with "Dearest Pete" and work up gradually to "Pete, my darling" because that seemed to her to be the most loving, the most tender, the most romantic: the one with the sound of real love echoing round the saying of it when it was spoken.

Down in the kitchen, a radio voice was talking at Dad while he got the tea ready. All Marion's life he had grumbled about being both a father and a mother to her and when she was small she had felt that he was cross with her. Perhaps, she used to think in those days, perhaps it was my fault that Mum died. In the last few years, though, she had realized that Dad enjoyed both the grumbling and the cooking, ironing and cleaning. It gave him pleasure to keep things, as he said, "shipshape and Bristol fashion". Wasn't he one of the best postmen the GPO had ever had? Thirty-five years and no letter ever mislaid or wrongly delivered. I should go down and lay the table, thought Marion. Help him a bit more, but at least it's an easy tea tonight. Steak pies, with baked potatoes and stewed apples. Pies were ten pence off today for staff. There were advantages to working in a supermarket.

Marion looked round her room, waiting for inspiration. What would Sue say if she could walk in here this minute? No pin ups, just pictures cut from magazines and stuck up on the wall in a kind of patchwork: pictures of lambs and cats and small puppies with ribbons round their necks, country cottages and the tropical beaches that went with advertisements for white rum, whose colours couldn't possibly be real. No sea that Marion had ever set eyes on was that particular shade of transparent, light-filled turquoise. Pete's sea, the sea around the oil-rig, was grey, surely, up there in the cold: metallic and swelling, full of menace, fog drifting over the water, wreaths of mist obscuring the long, iron joints, the hard angles sticking up out of the ice-cold darkness of the waves.

> I think of you every minute, Marion wrote. I think of you in the middle of all that black water, and I wish that you could be here with me. Nothing that I do without you seems real, somehow. They all just go past me with their baked beans and their fish fingers and washing powder and chocolate biscuits, and my fingers punch the right figures on the till and I don't see them at all. I see you. When I go to bed at night I think of you, and of all the marvellous fun we had while you were still here. Please write to me whenever you can. I'm just waiting to open a letter and hear your voice from far away when I read it. It's quite cold here, and I expect it's worse where you are . . .

Marion paused. Can I write it, she thought. Can I make the letters that will say it? She blushed and wrote: . . . I wish that I could warm you with my kisses.

Was that too much in the first letter? Was the letter long enough? How to end it? She could picture Peter reading the letter on the end of a hard bed covered with a scratchy red blanket, the kind of bed you might find in a hospital, or in the army. She could imagine what he looked like: dark, slightly wavy hair and blue eyes, the right eyes to look out over the miles of sea all around him. I must finish this letter, she thought. There ought to be some news, but were you allowed to put ordinary news in love letters, or only love, all on its own? She wrote quickly:

> I quite like the job at the supermarket, really. The manager is fat and jolly. He's called Mr Barlow, and there's a nice lady called Ena who makes tea for all of us, and a couple of lads behind the butcher's counter who fancy themselves, but don't worry, I'd never even look at someone else when I have you. There's also . . .

Should I? thought Marion, then: why not? Sue wouldn't mind.

> . . . a girl called Marion who works with me, and I think we'll get on quite well. I must stop now, because it's nearly teatime, but I'll write again very soon, and please write to me, because I miss you every minute.
>
> All my love and kisses,
>
> Sue

Marion put the letter in her bag, ready to take to work tomorrow. I hope Sue says its O.K., she thought. I don't fancy writing it all over again, like homework. I hope Peter likes it too. Marion sat on the bed and stared at the wallpaper (roses—so pretty—she had chosen it herself) without seeing it. She saw Pete. He had blue eyes, she knew, because Sue had told her, and the blue eyes were looking straight at her and they were smiling. It gave Marion a squashy feeling in her stomach.

"Tea's ready," shouted Dad, and the pips for seven o'clock pricked into her mind.

"Coming," Marion shouted back, and walked downstairs, trying to shake away her daydreams before she reached the kitchen. Oh, lucky Sue. Lucky, lucky Sue!

"Dad?" Marion said it without thinking. Her father was busy looking at the *Evening News*, as he did every evening after tea. He put the paper aside:

"Yes, love?"

"Dad, can I ask you something. I just wanted to know . . ." Marion took a deep breath, " . . . d'you reckon anyone'll ever fall in love with me?"

"I reckon they will, our Marion. You look just like your mum, and I fell in love with her, didn't I? You'll be away and married before too long."

"They're not exactly queuing up at the door, though, are they?"

"You're young yet, love. Only seventeen. Plenty of time for all that. And besides," he smiled, "you're not in the kind of job where you meet a lot of young men. Come and work for the GPO. Falling over lads down there, we are."

"I might, I suppose." Marion looked down. "But you couldn't say I was pretty, could you? Not honestly."

Her father thought for a moment. "Not exactly pretty, no. That isn't what I'd say. I'd say you were wholesome. That's it. Healthy and wholesome."

Wholesome. Marion considered the word as she washed up. Not pretty. Not attractive. Not sexy. Square and solid, brown hair cut in a fringe, bosom large without being enticing. Healthy. She thought: I feel as if I'm some kind of cake. If Sue were a cake, she'd be layers of feather-light pastry, with jam, and piped curls and flourishes of cream and a sprinkling of chocolate on top. Me, I'm brown and square and wholesome. A date and walnut loaf.

Sue was punching prices on to cans of hot dogs: twenty-three pence, over and over again. Even in her shop overall she looked glamorous, Marion thought. All that leg showing, all that shiny length of pale

beige nylon, and those strappy shoes. Mr Barlow and
Ena had had quite a giggle about those.

"Got to stand around a fair bit in this job, lass.
Those pretty little feet will be agony come half past
four," Mr Barlow's eyes were out on stalks. Sue had
smiled, glossy pink lips, smooth make up, brown eyes
like treacle, and said nothing and, as far as Marion
knew, her feet never bothered her at all.

Sue came nearer to the till. The shop was quiet
now, after the early morning rush.

"Have you got it?" she asked.

"Yes, it's in my bag. You can look and find it."

Sue grinned. "I'll just go and powder my nose, I
think. If Berty Barlow comes snooping around, tell
him anything that comes into your head."

"I hope it's O.K." said Marion.

"I don't know what I would have done without you,"
Sue said. "Honestly. I wouldn't know where to begin.
I'd just sit there and freeze up. It's really ever so nice
of you."

A woman approached the checkout with her
trolley.

"Wait till you see it before you say that," Marion
whispered, and turned her attention to the till. Sue
walked down the aisle towards the restroom. She
looked happy.

She hadn't looked happy when Marion had first seen
her. She'd been crying: blowing her nose into a lilac-
coloured tissue. She was sitting hunched up on one of
the two comfortable chairs in the cubby-hole where
the staff went for their breaks.

"Hello," said Marion. "I'm Marion. You must be
Sue. Mr Barlow said we'd got someone new starting
today."

Sue nodded through her tears.

"Pleased to meet you," she sniffed. "I'm sorry. I

80

mean, I'm sorry I'm like this. I'm not the weepy type normally but . . ."

Marion sat down, embarrassed.

"You can tell me about it. If you want to, that is. Or I'll just go away."

"No, no, please," Sue smiled weakly. "I'd like to tell somebody. I feel so alone."

"I'll make you a coffee, then, shall I?"

"Ta, love, I need one." Sue blew her nose. The tears had dried up a little. She sounded more cheerful. "It's Pete, you see. He's my boyfriend. We've been going together for ages. We're in love." She paused as though she expected Marion to say something. Marion filled the kettle and plugged it in. What was there to say? Sue continued:

"He's so . . . I can't explain it. We're like two halves of one thing, do you know what I mean?"

"Yes," said Marion. Well, it wasn't a lie. She'd read about such feelings. She'd seen all those lips on television, glued together in colour and close-up, all that breathing and sighing and staring into one another's eyes. You couldn't avoid it.

"Yes, I know what you mean."

"He's gone," said Sue, drama in her voice.

"Given you up, you mean?" Marion could hardly believe it. Even crying and sniffing, it was clear that Sue was pretty.

"No, it's worse than that." (What could be worse, Marion wondered.) "He's been posted to one of those bloody awful oil-rigs in the North Sea, and he won't be back till Christmas. Can you imagine anything so dreadful?"

Marion could. Christmas was only a few months away, after all, and then he'd be back. She said nothing, to be tactful.

"I miss him. I miss him so much. I feel as if a bit of me had been chopped off. I don't know how I'm going to get through the days. I don't really." Sue took a sip of her coffee, "And as for the nights . . ."

"You could write to him," Marion said quickly. She did not quite feel ready to hear about the nights. To her amazement, this simple remark sent Sue into new floods of tears.

"I'm sorry. What did I say? I didn't mean to make you cry again. What is it?"

"It's the letters. I promised Pete I'd write to him. I swore I would and I can't. I don't know how to begin. I never could string two words together, even at school. I can't even spell properly. I don't know what to do. If I don't write, he'll worry, you see. Think I've gone off with someone else. Oh, Marion, I wish you could help me!"

"Help you with the letter, you mean?" Marion was shocked. Would Sue (she hardly knew her, after all, had only met her a few minutes ago) really let her share the little bubble of love that sealed her and Pete up together and away from the rest of the world?

"I could help you with the spelling, I suppose. I was good at that at school."

"No, I mean," Sue was leaning forward now, anxious, "you could tell me what to say."

"But . . ."

"You've been in love, haven't you? You know what it's like." No, Marion wanted to answer. No, I've never been in love, I don't know anything about it really. Only what I imagine. Only what I dream about at nights. But Sue thinks I have. Sue thinks someone must have loved me as Pete loves her. Maybe they will . . . and if they did, then I'd know what to say. I can't tell her I've never been in love.

"Yes," she said finally, "I could probably tell you what to say. We could work something out together. During our dinner hour maybe."

"I've got an even better idea," Sue smiled. "Why

don't you write a letter, and then I'll copy it out and send it."

Marion could hardly find words. Did Sue really mean to hand her love over like an old parcel? Not have any say in it at all?

"What if," she said at last, "what if you don't like what I've written."

"Then I'll tell you, won't I? And we'll change it, won't we? I must get back to the shop now. They'll think I've disappeared."

"But what about Pete?"

"What about him?"

"Isn't it kind of . . . tricking him? Cheating him?"

"Not really," Sue grinned. "I'm the one that loves him, after all. You've never even seen him. And anyway," she winked, "what the eye doesn't see, the heart doesn't grieve over. See you later, then. Ta ever so much."

"That's O.K.," said Marion, but by then Sue had gone back into the shop.

II   September 17th

My darling Sue,

   I can't tell you what I felt like when I got your letter yesterday. I felt as if a little part of you was here with me. I keep your letter in the top pocket of my shirt, right near my heart, but I wish I could hold you. I wish it all the time. All the time I'm working and eating and chatting to my mates, I just want to feel you next to me, just want to hold you in my arms and forget about everything else.

Marion said: "Don't you feel funny about it, though?" She and Sue were arranging cauliflowers into an elegant pyramid on a shelf covered with plastic grass.

"Don't you feel funny about me reading all the letters he writes to you?"

"Not really," Sue shrugged. "Can't be helped, can it?"

"But all that stuff, it's sort of private, isn't it? Don't you feel embarrassed?"

"See worse on telly every night of the week, can't you, though? And in those fat books you're always reading, with busty ladies on the cover. I bet there's plenty in those."

"Yes, but that's made up, and this is real. It's different."

"It doesn't worry me, duck, so I shouldn't let it worry you." She looked at the cauliflower in her hand. "Can we get this one right on top there, or should I stick it round the back? It's a bit on the spotty side."

"Round the back," said Marion. Sue seemed to be behaving quite normally. Marion sighed. If someone had written a letter like that to her, she would quite probably be floating high above the assorted pickles and jams at this very moment on a pink, fluffy cloud, with a thousand invisible voices murmuring music into her ears.

October 5th

Pete, dearest,

I read in the paper about the gales where you are, and I wish I could magic you away and into the warm front room of our house. I love your letters. I love you. I have a special calendar, and I cross off each day when I go to bed, and then I lie there and think of you. I think of you so hard that after a while I can almost feel you kissing me. I dream about you . . .

October 13th

Sue, my beautiful Sue,

I dream about you, too. Every night, and during the day as well. I think about all the things we used to do. Remember the time when we were coming home from Stockport? Remember how we missed the last bus because I was kissing you—we didn't know where we

84

were, or what we were doing, did we? And remember the Christmas dance last year? I'll never forget that. I live it over in my mind all the time. You were so beautiful. I didn't think anyone could be so beautiful. Your skin was like white silk . . .

"Gone a bit overboard this time, hasn't he? Poor old Pete." Sue laughed. "I expect that's all they think about up there, all those lads together."

Marion blushed. "He misses you, that's all. He loves you. I think it's a lovely letter."

Sue wrinkled her nose. "All that bit about skin like silk, though. It isn't as if he'd seen all that much of it, really."

Marion looked away. Sue had never told her. Not exactly, and she didn't want to know, not everything, but now she asked tentatively, trying to match Sue's brisk tone of voice: "What's all this about the Christmas dance, then? Pete seems to think . . ."

"Pete!" Sue laughed. "He's just exaggerating. I tell you, it's the boredom. It makes them all sex-mad. It's a well-known fact. I spilled something all over my blouse, that's all. Just before we went out. And Pete . . . well, I went up to change, and you know . . . Dad and Mum were out, and I let him come up with me while I changed and then, well, there I was in my bra, and we kissed. That's all. Till I put another blouse on. It wasn't anything much. We were late for the dance as it was, so the whole thing only lasted five minutes. He's just made it seem much more important than it was, really."

All morning, Marion could not stop thinking about it. Thinking about hands, Pete's hands on bare skin, his lips touching bare skin. Sue's skin, thought Marion, Sue's skin, so why do I feel as if I'm the one, as if it all happened in my room, as if it had all happened to me?

November 22nd

Pete, my darling,

I bought your Christmas present today and I can't wait to give it to you. I can't believe it. It's only one more month and then we'll be together. I'm so happy. I walk around the shop on air and Berty Barlow says I've got stars in my eyes, and I have and they're shining just for you. I keep your letters tied up with a ribbon, just like they do in stories, because I love them so much. Every time I get one, I feel happy. When I think of seeing you again, I get dizzy. I play a film over and over again in my mind of me meeting you at the airport. I can close my eyes whenever I want to, and just see it: I'll run and run to meet you, and hug you, and hold you close, and we'll kiss and kiss and never stop . . .

December 14th

Sue, my darlingest, lovely Sue,

I can't write much this time because I'm so hear to coming home that my hand shakes every time I pick up a pen. I've got a present for you, and something to ask you. Something important. Can you guess?

Marion couldn't sleep. She looked at her watch. Two o'clock. I won't be fit for anything tomorrow, she thought, and it's the Christmas booze-up at the shop. She switched on the light and got out of bed. From the top drawer of her chest of drawers she took a pad and went to fetch her biro from the handbag hanging on the back of the door. Then she got back into bed, balancing the pad on her knees and began to write:

Dear Pete,

You're coming home tomorrow and I can't bear it. Sue will be so happy, but for me it's like the end of a long dream. All these months while I've been writing these letters for her, I've been putting myself in her place, feeling all the love she feels, remembering things that I never really knew about in the first place. Things like what it feels like to kiss you, the way you talk and smile, and what your hands are like when they hold mine. Now it's all got to stop and it's as though something wonderful is going to end. Those letters from you, it got so I almost believed they were really written to me. I pretended that they were. It made me so happy. I don't even know what you look like and I love you. There it is. I've said it. It's like falling in love with a ghost. Sue showed me those pictures you sent, but they were so small and faraway and you were all wearing those funny oil-rig hats, I couldn't really see you. I've got my own picture in my head and that's good enough. I don't know if you'll come into the shop. I want you to and I don't want you to. I'd like to see you, of course, but also I wish that you could keep on being a lovely dream that I had.

All my love,

Marion

Marion put the pad on the bedside table and turned out the light. For a while she lay staring at the wall. Then quickly she sat up and fumbled in the darkness and found the sheet on which she had written. She pulled it out of the pad with shaking fingers and tore it across and across again until it was a pile of tiny white flakes all over her bed. Then she buried her head in the pillow and the tears came and came, flowing out of her as if there was to be no end to them, ever.

III

"Marion! Marion . . ." Sue was beckoning her from the till.

"Yes?"

"He's done it."

"What?"

"He's asked me. Pete, I mean. To marry him."

"Oh," Marion forced herself to smile. "That's lovely. Congratulations."

"It's all thanks to you really. Those letters, that's what did it."

87

"Nonsense. I'm glad I could help. When will it be?"

"Easter, we hope. We're going to have an engagement party. You'll come, won't you? You must meet him. After all, you know him as well as anyone."

"Yes. Thanks. That'd be lovely." Marion turned away and began to pile up assorted biscuits in red and green tins, holly-decked and dotted about with fat robins in honour of Christmas. I can't bear it, she thought. I won't go. I'll be sick. I don't want ever to see him. I can't. I won't. I don't want to. I'll have to buy a new dress. A tiny, half-formed thought rose at the back of Marion's mind. A party. She didn't get asked to many. Perhaps there would be someone there who would make her forget. Perhaps she would see someone across the room. I'll have to go, she thought. Sue'll be ever so hurt if I don't go. And Pete . . . I want to see him. Just the once.

Party voices came floating through the air to Marion, who stood tucked in a corner between the sideboard and the wall.

"Make a lovely bride."

"He's a lucky man."

"Once they're married."

"Only twenty-five quid, and that was on account of knowing Frank who used to work there."

"Shouldn't wonder, but it's different now, isn't it?"

"Not real velvet, you see. More the synthetic."

"Another of those?"

"Peanuts?"

"A bit of all right."

Marion sipped her punch and looked down at her new dress. Burgundy, that's what the colour was called. The lady in the shop had said. That sounded lovely, but to Marion it looked, in this light, like what? Old plums? Dried blood? Something awful anyway. What did it matter? This was a stupid, mixed up kind of party anyhow, with all Sue's elderly relatives and all her friends pushed together into two tiny rooms, with the heating turned full on. Marion had hoped for a disco maybe, or else a smart hotel, but this . . . well, once weddings were in the air, they all came out of the woodwork: aunts and cousins you hadn't seen in years, bringing engagement presents. She tried to imagine what her own party would be like when (if) someone wanted to marry her. Dad and his cronies, and Gran and who else? Ena? Mr Barlow? Sue? It won't be the same as this anyway because I haven't got a mother. Sue's mother is like Sue, only old. Powder blue jersey dress, and high strappy shoes like the ones Sue wears. Can you inherit your taste in shoes from your mum? Marion looked down at her low-heeled patent leather pumps and sighed. For a moment she had the strong feeling of being at a funeral.

It wasn't the shoes. Not them, nor the dress, nor the old aunts and uncles, nothing like that. It was Pete. Marion searched for him in the crowded room, and found him at last, talking to Sue's dad near the window. He looked, Marion shivered, he looked insignificant. Small (and what was wrong with being small, for heaven's sake? Where had she got the idea that he would tower above her?) with a narrow kind of face, and blue eyes, true enough, but a washed out shade of blue, and too close together anyway. He had thin lips, hardly any lips at all, really, and when he smiled his mouth made a square, and in that square were lots of other smaller squares of teeth.

"This is Marion," Sue had said.

"I've heard a lot about you," he smiled. "Sue wrote to me. Nice to meet you."

"Nice to meet you, too." Marion whispered and turned away because she couldn't bear to be there when something died, when all the love that she had bottled up inside herself evaporated like liquid left out in the sun.

Later, she tried to be sensible. It's no skin off my nose, she decided finally, after a second glass of punch. He wasn't even mine. Nothing to do with me at all. Why should I care? It's Sue's problem. But how can she love him? She could have anyone she wanted and she chooses him. Well, all right, so he doesn't look like much, but you shouldn't judge by appearances. I mean, who'd come near me, the date and walnut loaf in the dried blood dress? And yet, I could love someone. I bet there are loads of people I could get on with. I'm all right. Sue likes me . . . lots of people like me . . . when I was helping out at the meat counter the other week, Jim said we should go bowling one night. I don't know that I'd fancy that too much, but he did mention it, that's something.

"Marion?"

"Oh! Hello." It was Pete.

"Your glass is empty. Can I get you another of whatever it was?"

"No, thanks, Pete. I'm a bit tipsy already."

How strange to be talking right to him, and not to feel anything. It's all gone: love, jealousy, longing. It's as if it never happened. In a way, it's a relief, but how empty, how dull the world looks all of a sudden.

"What about something soft, then? A Coke, with lots of ice."

"That'd be nice."

"I'll just go through to the kitchen and get it."

"I might as well come with you. Can I? I'm nearly fainting with the heat in here."

"Sure. Come on."

There was no one in the kitchen.

"Let's get some ice," said Pete.

Oh, look at me, thought Marion, look at me, all alone in the kitchen with the man of my dreams.

90

Maybe if I spill Coke all over this dress, I could take it off and he might kiss me, kiss my skin like white silk. Marion giggled.

"I really am a little tipsy," she said.

"This'll sort you out. Here, sit down."

"O.K. It's a bit noisy in there, isn't it?"

"Right. And all those people. Not that I've got anything against Sue's family, mind. No, it's not that . . ."

"There's rather a lot of them, though," said Marion.

"Right. Nice to be able to have a proper chat with someone. Sue thinks a lot of you. She told me. Going to ask you to be her bridesmaid, only don't tell her I told you. She wants to ask you herself.'

"Go on," Marion laughed. "Can you see me in cream organza with primroses in my hair? Sue must be joking."

"No, I don't think so," Pete smiled. "You'll look great, don't worry."

Did he really think so, or was he being polite? Either way, one gold star for Pete. He's tactful, anyway.

"She's ever so happy now you're back," said Marion. "She used to long for your letters."

"And I just used to count the days till hers came. I did, honestly."

"I expect they made you feel closer to her somehow."

"They did. That's it exactly. They were marvellous letters. I can tell you that. Terrific, really."

"Well, from what Sue said, your letters were pretty terrific, too."

Pete blushed. Why is he blushing, Marion wondered. And why isn't he saying anything? He's looking all around as if to make sure there's no one here. He's leaning across the table . . .

Pete said: "I'm going to tell you something, Marion,

91

really don't ever tell Sue. I've had it a bit on my conscience, really, for the last few months. You won't tell her, will you?"

"No, really. I promise I won't."

"I don't think she'd ever trust me again if she knew."

"What is it?"

He sighed, and looked down at his fingernails. "It's the letters. I never wrote them. Not one. Not even a bit of them."

"Then . . . ?"

"Another bloke wrote them for me. I can't string two words together, not really. He wrote them to help me out, like. He's a good chap. Name of Tom Granger. He'd never let on. But it feels funny. Like sharing Sue with another man in a way." Pete shook his head.

"I don't think that's so dreadful," said Marion after a pause. "I mean if he hadn't written them, then Sue wouldn't have got them, would she? And that would have made her miserable."

"D'you think it's all right then? I didn't know what to do when that first letter came. I tried to write but . . . well, then Tom helped me out. But I do love her. The letters don't make any difference to that."

"No, of course they don't. They don't matter a bit. Really."

"I feel better now I've talked to you, though. I feel I've kind of got it off my chest."

"I won't say a word." Marion smiled. "Hadn't we better go back?"

"Yeah, maybe it'll thin out a bit in there, now it's getting late."

One of Sue's uncles gave Marion a lift home.

"Is that you, Marion?" Dad was still awake, then. Waiting up for her. A mother and father to her, all her life.

"Yes, Dad. Only me."

"Had a good party, then?" (The voice cotton woolly. He'd taken out his false teeth.)

"Smashing."

"Good girl. Sleep tight, then."

"Don't let the bugs bite." She said the words without thinking, just as she had said them almost every every night of her life.

In her room, she took off her dress and hung it up carefully. She stroked her own shoulders. Silken skin? Maybe. Maybe someone would think it was. Look at Sue and Pete. Look at Sue, and oh, just look at poor old Pete, and Sue loved him, really did, was going to marry him, wasn't she? You must get a magic lens in front of your eyes when you fall in love, that makes everybody beautiful.

In the dark, lying in bed in the dark, it was safe to think of it. Safe to think. Tom Granger. A new name? An unknown face. What did he look like, and did it matter? For months, she and Tom had written all those letters, poured out all that love. Marion smiled. Tom would probably be lonely up there now that Pete had left. Tom, all alone in the icy fields, furrows of water, leaves of mist clinging to the metal branches of the rig, ice forming on the huge bolts and nails, on all the sharp edges open to the sky. Tom, with his locker full of ... what? Pin-ups? Books? Cards? Maybe he had someone at home. And then again, maybe not. Maybe he would welcome a friend, a penfriend. That would be a way to begin, as a penfriend. It was worth trying surely? What harm could it do? I've even got the address. I'll never forget that address. Dear Tom, you don't know me, but I'm a friend of Pete's and Sue's, and I wonder whether . . . Marion fell asleep, still smiling.

The Poppycrunch Kid

"O.K, my darling, let me just explain what I want you to do, and then we'll rehearse it a couple of times before we try it on camera. Right?" Melanie nodded. Bill, the producer, was being nice to her. Much nicer than he was to everyone else in the studio. He shouted at them sometimes. Swore even, but he never shouted or swore at her, because she was the Poppycrunch Kid and Very Important. Melanie pulled her skirt down and fluffed out her bunches. Were her ribbons still all right? Mum said she was a Star. It was hard to believe. Two weeks ago, she'd lined up with a whole lot of other little girls, and they'd chosen her out of all of them to be the Poppycrunch Kid. Some of the girls had been much prettier, too.

"But your little girl, Mrs White," Bill had said to her mother and right in front of her, too, "has such zest, such life, such—how shall I put it? Spice, that's the word, the right word—the others were all—d'you know what I mean?—flavourless. And you see, what the makers do want to promote more than anything, is an image of Brightness, Vigour and Intelligence . . . the concept is one of Life, you see, rather than an unreal kind of prettiness. I'm sure Melanie will be Perfection Itself."

Melanie didn't understand why the sight of her trampolining, skipping, sliding down a helter-skelter, leaping out of bed or doing a tap-dance, dressed always in a red T-shirt and a short white skirt, should make everyone stop buying their favourite cereal and

94

turn to Poppycrunch instead. She wasn't going to eat it.

"But you must," said Mrs White in desperation.

"Why?"

"It's called Brand Loyalty. They're paying you enough money. You might at least do them the favour of eating their cereal. I think it's lovely."

"It's horrible. All hard. I could think up a few truthful slogans, like 'Tear your gums on a Poppy-crunch,' or something."

"But you're going to be famous, Melanie. Don't you want to be famous? Isn't that what you've always wanted? You've said so over and over again. 'I want to be a star' you said."

"It's not being a star—not advertising cereal. I want to be in a proper show, like 'Annie'. I wish I'd got into 'Annie'."

"You were too tall. I keep telling you. And besides, millions more people see advertisements than ever walk into a theatre. Maybe someone'll spot you. You never know. Anyway, it's good exposure, you've got to say that for it."

That was the only reason Melanie could think of for doing it. Someone, someone from Hollywood even, would see her trampolining or skipping or whatever, and decide, right there on the spot, that she was exactly what he needed for his very next film, and whisk her far away in a jet to be a real actress, a child star.

"Are you ready, Melanie?" Bill cooed.

"Yes."

"Right. Let's start then."

Melanie skipped towards the trampoline (red, with 'Poppycrunch' written on it in white letters) leaped on to it and began to bounce, singing at the same time the silly little tune they'd given her to learn, and smiling widely enough to crack her face open:

Full of goodness
Full of fun
Poppycrunch
The chewy one!

Three things at once—it was harder to do than it looked, like patting your head with one hand while rubbing the other hand over your stomach in circles. Melanie had to do it four times before she'd got it just right. At last, Bill was satisfied.

"Great, my love," he said. "Absolutely scrumptious. Now as soon as you've got your breath back, we'll film it. O.K?"

"Yes, said Melanie. The thought of doing it all over again on film made the butterflies start up in her stomach, just as though she were about to act in front of a real, live audience. It was silly. There was only Bill, and Christine, his assistant and some lighting men and sound men, and her mother in the corner of the studio, and of course, the cameras. Melanie had never thought about the cameras before. They were like robots: huge square tall things on long metal legs that slid across the floor trailing thick black cables like snakes. You had to look at them quite hard to spot the men who were working them. The cameras had lenses for eyes sticking out towards you. Never, never looking at anything else except you. Melanie shivered.

"Now, Melanie, I don't want you to think about the cameras at all. Just forget about them. They're not there, all right? I want you to be quite, quite natural, my love and Reg and Ben here will do all the work—focus on you like mad, all the time. Give Melanie a little wave, lads, just to show her you're there."

Arms came out of the sides of the camera and waved. It was as if the cameras themselves were waving at her.

"Right-o, my dears," said Bill. "If you're all ready I'm going to do my Cecil B. De Mille routine . . . Roll'em!"

Melanie sang and smiled and trampolined. She sang and smiled and trampolined seven times. They had to do seven 'takes' before everything came out exactly as Bill wanted it.

"That's fantastic, Melanie. Really fantastic. it's not unknown for me to do a dozen 'takes'. Great. It's going to look great. Come and see."

Melanie went. It seemed like a lot of other advertisements to her. She was quite pleased with how high she'd managed to jump on the trampoline, but it was all over so quickly—a few seconds, that was all. Tomorrow they would do leaping out of bed. That shouldn't be so tiring. Suddenly Melanie felt exhausted, unable to think straight. The silly words and silly tune of the Poppycrunch jingle had got stuck in her head and wound round her other thoughts like thin strings of chewing-gum that wouldn't come off.

> Full of goodness
> Full of fun
> Poppycrunch
> The chewy one.

Round and round in her head.

That night, Melanie dreamed that Camera One was in her bedroom. Standing in the doorway and looking at her room. And there was a wind. It blew all round the room and sucked the furniture and the toys and all her dolls and clothes and the pictures from the walls till everything was whirling round and round in a spiral that started out huge and got smaller and smaller until at last it vanished right into the lens of the camera and then the walls weren't there any longer either, just a bed with her in it, and Camera

One floating about in a bright, colourless space that went on and on for ever and never stopped.

"Christine," said Melanie, "do you think you could ask Bill something for me?"

"Of course, poppet. Anything you like. What is it?"

"Well, it's a bit embarrassing . . ."

"Go on, you can tell me. Can't you? You know I'll help."

"Yes, I know, but it's so stupid."

"Never mind, it's obviously worrying you, so go ahead and tell me. You'll feel better, honestly."

"It's Camera One. I'm scared of it."

"Scared of a camera?" Christine smiled. "But why love? What do you think it can do to you?"

"I don't know. I dreamed about it, that's all."

"You're overwrought, my love. Don't worry. You're frightened because it's new to you. It's . . . well . . . it's a bit like stage fright, only different. Come and have a look. I'll get Reg to let you touch it and get to know it so you'll never be frightened of it again."

Reg was understanding.

"It's only a kind of mechanical eye, love. That's all. Metal and glass and stuff that can see. It is a bit like magic, I grant you, because it's a clever old thing. Does a lot that your eyes and mine can't do—it can give back the pictures that it sees and show them all over again, but it's not magic, see. It's called Technology. Nothing to be scared of, honestly."

"No. I suppose not," said Melanie. "I'm being stupid."

"No, no love," said Reg. "It's not stupid. I'll tell you something. There are primitive tribes in the world, New Guinea and places like that, and they don't even like snapshots being taken of them. They reckon every time a photo gets taken, it steals away a bit of their soul. That's their superstition, see? Bet you've had a million snapshots taken of you since you were born, and you're none the worse for it, are you? Neither is anyone else. So don't worry, O.K?"

"O.K," said Melanie and went over to the beautiful bed that had been set out on the studio floor. I wish Reg hadn't told me that, she thought. About those people in New Guinea. I know it's only a superstition, but I wish he hadn't told me, all the same.

"Action!" Bill shouted and Melanie bounded out of bed, grinning and singing:

> Ready for work
> Ready for play.
> Start every day
> The Poppycrunch way!

She did it ten times. It wasn't her fault. They had to find some way of getting the pillow into the picture with her. The famous Poppycrunch symbol was printed on the pillowslip, and of course, it had to be seen, or what was the point?

There were three more films to make. The helter-skelter was fun. A very short tune and not a lot of words:

> Bite it
> Munch it
> Poppycrunch it!

Also, Melanie didn't care how many times she had to come sliding down till the timing was just perfect. She was getting used to filming, beginning to enjoy it, just as Bill and Christine and Reg had said she would. She sang the songs at home, all the time. At school, she showed her friends exactly what she had to do. She found it very hard to concentrate on her work, because her head was full of bouncy music and bright slogan words and they seemed to be pushing whatever it was she was supposed to be thinking about into some corner of her mind where she could never quite reach it. Miss Hathersage, her teacher, asked her one day:

"Melanie, dear, what are seven nines?"

Melanie's mind raced. Seven nines? What were nines? Full of goodness . . . Nine whats? Sevens— full of fun . . .

"I don't know, please, Miss."

"Of course you know, dear. You did the nine times table last year. Now come on, dear, think."

Melanie thought . . . the chewy one. She closed her eyes . . . white skirt flying . . . jump as high as you can . . . Poppycrunch . . . ready for work . . . ready for play . . .

"I can't think, Miss, I'm sorry." Melanie hung her head.

"Very well, then. Sarah, some people have let being on television go to their heads, I can see. What are seven nines?"

"Sixty three, Miss Hathersage."

"Quite right. Sixty three. Do you remember now, Melanie?"

"Yes, Miss." But I don't remember, Melanie thought. I don't and I must. Seven nines are sixty three, sixty three. Even as she thought it, she felt the numbers slipping away, losing their meaning, losing themselves over the precipices that seemed to lie at the very edges of her mind.

That night, Melanie dreamed that she was reading. Camera One was looking at her as she turned the pages of her book. She watched as the words flew off the page and drifted on to the floor, millions of tiny black letters, all over the rug. She tried to pick them up and put them back into the book in the right

100

order, but they fell out of her hands, and crumbled like ash when she touched them.

"What's the matter, love?" said Christine. "You're looking a bit pale today. Are you tired? I bet you are, you know. You've had to do all these films one on top of the other, and never a rest in between. Bill," she raised her voice. "I'm going to take Melanie back to Make-Up. I think she needs a spot more rouge, don't you?"

Bill came and stood in front of Melanie, frowning.

"Yes, darling. Oh, and ask them at the same time to see if they can get rid of those shadows under her eyes. You've not been looking after yourself, love, now have you? You must, you know. That's what we're paying you for—to look healthy, full of life. Run along with Christine now and see what Make-Up can do for you."

Melanie lay in the make-up chair listening to Christine's voice which seemed to come from very far away.

"I don't think you're getting enough sleep, love. Honestly. Are you?"

"I start every day the Poppycrunch way . . ." Melanie whispered.

"Are you sleeping properly, Melanie?"

"I dream a lot," Melanie said.

"Bad dreams?" Christine sounded concerned.

"No. Poppycrunch dreams. Just me and Camera One."

"You dream about Camera One? I thought you'd got over all that. You don't seem nervous in front of the cameras at all. What do you dream?"

"I dream I'm singing and I don't know what comes next and then Camera One looks at me and I know . . . I know what to do if it looks at me. It tells me what to say."

101

"What does it tell you to say?"

"Words. Tunes.

> Poppycrunch for you
> Poppycrunch for me
> Poppycrunch for breakfast
> Poppycrunch for tea."

"Those are today's words," Christine sounded worried. "I'll have a word with your Mum and Bill after the filming today. I reckon you need a damn good rest. You're just exhausted. Tell me," she added as though something had just occurred to her, "what do you do at home? For relaxation? Do you read any books?"

"No. I stopped. I used to like it, but then I stopped."

"Why did you stop?"

Melanie looked up. "Because I can't remember what the story's about any more. I can't hold the story in my head. It's as though," Melanie hesitated, "as though my head's full of deep, black water and everything that goes in it just sinks under the water and won't come up to the surface again."

"Right," said Christine. "See if you can get through this afternoon's filming and then I'll have a word with them. It won't be long now."

"Oh," Melanie's face lit up, "you don't have to do that. Don't worry. I love it. I love the filming. I love Camera One. I know all the words. And all the tunes. And just what to do." Melanie skipped all the way back to the studio, singing the Poppycrunch jingle for today. Christine followed more slowly. All hell was going to break loose when she told Bill. That was for sure.

"Christine, my beloved," said Bill, "you have clearly taken leave of your senses. Let me go over what you've just said. Melanie White is exhausted and

102

overwrought and you think we should scrap the whole of the last film. Is that right?"

"Yes," said Christine quietly. "That's quite right."

"Well, now, I'll answer you as calmly as I can because I don't want a row. I'll try and go over the points one by one so that you understand. First, the Poppycrunch commercials are the hottest thing I've done since the Suckamints Campaign, and you know how many prizes that won. Sales of Poppycrunch are up twenty per cent in the last two weeks. It follows, therefore, that the makers are not going to look kindly on someone jeopardizing their profits. Second, this last film is the biggest and most important of all. It's much longer. It's got fifteen other kids in it besides Melanie, doing things in the background while she dances at the front, and each one of those kids has to be cossetted and looked after, not to mention paid. It has a ten-piece band that has to be cossetted and looked after as much as the kids and paid even more. We've booked studio time. We've rehearsed, and we've even paid through our noses to be allowed to use the tune of 'Sweet Georgia Brown'. So I ask you, how can I cancel? Go on. Tell me. I'm anxious to know."

Christine said nothing. Bill went on:

"What do you think, Mrs White? Would you be in favour of cancelling? Do you think Melanie is exhausted and overwrought?"

"Well," Mrs White considered. "She is a bit tired, naturally. I mean, we all are, aren't we? I am myself and I just sit here and watch. But Melanie would be ever so put out if it was cancelled. I do know that. Eats, drinks and sleeps Poppycrunch, she does. Obsessed with it. Sings those tunes all day and every day. If her friends come over she teaches them all the words, tells them everything she has to do. They just play Poppycrunch games. Well, they don't come

103

round much any more. I reckon they're fed up and I have said to her she ought to ease up a bit, but it's as if she can't. It's as if, I can't explain it really, as if there's no room left inside her for anything else."

"Then don't you think we should stop it before it's too late?" Christine said. "You're her mother. You can see. You've said yourself—she's obsessed."

"Yes, but," Mrs White looked down at her hands, embarrassed, 'I'm sure it'll be all right when all the filming's finished. It is only one more after all, isn't it?"

"Right," said Bill. "Only one more. So that's decided. I'm really glad we were able to agree, Mrs White. It's going to be a corker, this last film. Wait and see."

That night, Melanie dreamed again. Her mother, and her school friends and Bill and Christine were all standing in the television studio and one by one they went up and stood in front of Camera One. Each one of them went right up to the camera and said something and then they got smaller and smaller until they disappeared altogether. Then she went and stood right up close to Camera One and said "I'm the Poppycrunch Kid" and then she got larger and larger until she took up all the space in the studio and Camera One kept looking at her and she kept growing and growing until she was all there was left in the whole world.

Melanie knew all the words, of course, but they were written up on a big board for the benefit of the fifteen little girls who had to jiggle up and down in the background while Melanie tap-danced at the front. The only words Melanie had to sing were: "The Poppycrunch Kid'. She had to sing it six times and then the film ended with her singing the last three lines all on her own. This is the best of all, thought Melanie. A real band, not a tape, all those other children, and that tune, so much more zingy than the others.

"Here we go, kids," said Bill. "Let's try it from the top."

The saxophone played an introduction and the children dutifully began jigging about and singing as Melanie went into the dance routine:

> "Who's that kid with the bouncy step?"
> "The Poppycrunch Kid!"
> (this was Melanie's line.)
> "Who's the girl who's full of pep?"
> "The Poppycrunch Kid!"
> "Who's got the other kids all sewn up?"
> "The Poppycrunch Kid!"
> "The Poppycrunch Kid!"
> "You said it, you did!"
>
> "Who's got the shiny eyes and hair?"
> "The Poppycrunch Kid!"
> "When fun happens, who's right there?"
> "The Poppycrunch Kid!"
> "The cereal this kid eats
> Is the kind with the built-in treats . . .
> Nuts and honey
> For your money
> Be a Poppycrunch Kid!"

It was much harder, Melanie decided, filming with all the others. So many things went wrong. Someone's hair ribbon coming undone, someone looking the wrong way, a wrong note from one of the band: any one of a thousand things could happen and did happen and they had to start again. Melanie didn't mind. She fixed her eyes on Camera One's magic eye, and felt as though just looking at it, she was falling and falling down into a place where there was nothing except light and music and tapping feet and words that circled in her brain and didn't puzzle her or worry her or make her think: words that comforted her, made her feel safe, magic words that were all she needed to say. Spells, incantations that were so powerful they could empty your head of every other thought . . .

"Twenty takes," said Bill. "I'm finished. Completely and utterly finished, Christine, and that's the truth."

"You're not the only one," said Christine. "Did you see Melanie?"

"She's a real trouper, that kid. I mean she even looked as if she were loving every minute of it all the way through."

"She was," said Christine. "It's not normal. How's she going to go back to ordinary life. I worry about it sometimes."

"Don't be silly, love. It's not as though she's the first child ever to appear on a commerical. We've got another lot coming in tomorrow to audition for the crisps film. Lord help us."

"No, but she was different."

"Bloody good on camera, though," said Bill, "And that's what counts in the end, isn't it?"

"Oh, yes," Christine agreed dully. "The camera just loved her. You could see that."

On the studio floor, Camera One stood amid its cables with a plastic cover over it to protect it from the dust. It's work was finished. Until tomorrow. Until the next child was chosen.

"Hello, dear," said the doctor. "And how are you today?"

"Full of goodness, full of fun," said Melanie.

"You're looking much better, I must say. Have you thought about what I asked you yesterday?"

Melanie nodded.

"Good girl. That's a good girl. Now. Tell me who you are. Tell me your name."

"The Poppycrunch Kid."

"No, Melanie. That's not your name, is it?" Your name is Melanie White. Believe me. Say it."

"Melanie White."

"There, doesn't that sound better? Are you going to play today, Melanie?"

"Ready for work, ready for play, start every day the Poppycrunch way."

"You could play outside today. It's a beautiful day."

"I'm full of pep . . ."

"I'm glad to hear it. Your mother will be coming to see you today. That'll be nice, won't it? You love having visitors, don't you?"

"Bite it, munch it, Poppycrunch it . . ."

"I'll see you tomorrow then, Melanie." The doctor stood up. "I'll look in after breakfast."

"Poppycrunch for breakfast," said Melanie and turned over to look at the wall.

I've got shiny eyes and hair and when fun happens I'm right there, but they took Camera One away. Maybe if I'm extra good, it'll come back. I'm the kid with the bouncy step. That man. He's the producer. But I've got the other kids all sewn up. They can't let anyone else be the Poppycrunch Kid. They put me here to see. To see if I really am the Poppycrunch Kid and if I'm not, then they'll choose someone else. But I'm the one. The Poppycrunch Kid, you said it, you did—when fun happens who's right there, the cereal this kid eats, is the one with the built-in treats, nuts and honey, bite it, munch it, Poppycrunch it.

She could hear them at visting time.

"Look, Herbert," said the lady's voice. "Isn't that

the kid who was on the telly? You know, that Poppy-cereal stuff. I'm sure it's her."

"Don't be silly," said Herbert. "She was pretty—full of life. That kid looks half dead to me."

I'm not, she thought, I'm full of fun, full of goodness . . . Poppycrunch for me . . .

The Graveyard Girl

I'm Teresa Wignall. I remember. I do remember that, though I've forgotten other things. I remember pieces of my life, but they're fading. There's a face looking worried, which is my mother's face, I think, but I can't call it to mind properly any more. There are children. They'd be my brothers and sisters, I suppose, but their names are gone and what they looked like, too. Sometimes, I'll see a child and the beginnings of a memory will stir in me like a dead leaf blowing, but it's gone. It's all gone. I drift about here and watch the seasons turning. There are roses in the summer and leaves in autumn to cover the graves and pile into small hills along the paths. And behind the wall, there is the school. The seasons turn and I watch. All the children. They come in the morning. If the windows are open, I can hear them singing. I can see them jumping in the playground, skipping, chanting rhymes:

> Here comes the doctor,
> Here comes the nurse,
> Here comes the lady,
> With the alligator purse . . .

The children make the windows pretty. In winter, they stick paper snowflakes all over them. Lambs and flowers in the spring. Orange and yellow and red leaves in the autumn and then it's winter again. Round and round they go, the seasons. The children come and go. Sometimes, they are gone for weeks and then they come back again. They come back, and grow and learn and play and talk. I sit on the wall and watch them. I lean over

109

the wall and listen to stories floating out of the windows. I wish I could be like them. I remember stories from before. At Sunday School there was a lady with a long dress and a hat trimmed with fur who read to us from a big book. I sit on the wall and wait. Sometimes, one of the children looks in my direction, but they don't see me. I have waited so long. Soon, soon I will be ready. I will be brave enough. I will go. I will. Go.

George Macmahon has been the caretaker of St Peter's School for many years. He is a man devoted to shiny brass, shiny linoleum and shiny paintwork. He is the enemy of litter, dust, dirt and scratches on the tops of desks. He sweeps the playground every morning. There are always leaves blown across from the churchyard beyond the school wall, not to mention all the stuff the kids leave lying around during term time, and drifts of yellow bus tickets that blow in from the main road. George Macmahon is not a religious man, but he likes St Peter's church next door. A no-nonsense building: tall with a high, square tower and a clock that you can rely on. No noisy chimes to interrupt your train of thought. The graveyard is a credit to Mr Wiles, the gardener and handyman. No one's been buried there now for years and years. The corpses seem to go down to the huge Municipal Cemetery now, but the old graves in St Peter's, with their blackened stones and chipped urns and mossy angels, are all kept as tidy as possible. All the grass is shaved as close as you please and tasteful roses, and discreet bushes of hydrangea, forsythia and suchlike, have been planted to cheer the place up a bit.

Mrs Macmahon, who used to do school dinners in the old days but can't any more, on account of her bad legs, is of the opinion that it's asking for trouble, putting a school playground right beside a graveyard. Morbid, that's what she thinks it is, and anyway, some of those kids, you never know what they'll get up to. As for Mr Macmahon, if he's told her once, he's told her a thousand times: "Never take any notice of it, that I've seen. Never. Been past it so often that they've stopped seeing it. Part of the furniture, that's all." Mrs Macmahon shakes her head, purses her lips and pours herself another cup of tea. Sometimes she speaks and sometimes she doesn't bother and just thinks to herself: "Nevertheless. Them's dead people in there. Them's graves. Doesn't matter how old they are. Graves and kids together shouldn't be allowed. There might be ghosts."

Mrs Macmahon also believes that ghosts are more likely to be found in old, disused graveyards. You can imagine a ghost coming to haunt you from a hundred years back or thereabouts, but to think of poor Ada Partridge, taken a month ago with pneumonia, flitting around like a blessed bit of fog—well, that was ridiculous. Mrs Macmahon wouldn't, couldn't credit it. Ada a ghost! The thought made her giggle.

George Macmahon does not believe in ghosts at all. He's very firm on the subject. He says: "I should know, shouldn't I? Worked next door to gravestones all my life and never a glimmer of anything strange. Nothing." He tells anyone who'll listen. "You'll see people pass through of course. Only natural from time to time ... walking about. That's ordinary mortals. Nothing," as he puts it privately, "to get into a lather about. People, same as you and me."

The first day of term. The first day of a new school year. Mrs Pike, in charge of Junior Two, is wearing a fluffy new cardigan with pearl buttons. The school smells clean. Clean rolled-up socks in all the pump-bags. Nice fresh painting overalls smelling of washing powder. No pictures are up yet in the corridors, after the summer holidays. The children are good.

111

Still quiet. Excited. There are piles of new exercise books to be given out. Extra sharp pencils. Empty lockers, not a single sweet paper lurking. No crisp bags blowing about in the playground. Not yet.

Mrs Pike says: "Good morning, Junior Two. Sit down in your places, please and let's see who we are. Hello, Susan dear. And Kevin. Well," she smiles, "there are lots of faces here I know already."

"Please, Miss," Wendy's hand waves in the air. "Please, Miss."

"Quiet, everyone," Mrs Pike says firmly. "What is it, dear?"

"Please, Miss, there's a new girl. She's called Teresa."

"Thank you, dear. Now let us all sit down and I shall take the register and then we shall see who is and who isn't here."

The children are quiet. the rocking up-and-down chanting of names, the repeated "Yes Miss" thirty times over, settles over the room like a lullaby. Mrs Pike closes the register.

"Please, Miss," says Wendy. "You haven't said Teresa."

"Well, Teresa," says Mrs Pike, "stand up, dear, and let's look at you."

A very thin, small child with long, pale hair stands up at the back of the room. Mrs Pike thinks: whatever will they send them wearing next? Fancy such a long and fussy dress for school. And none too clean by the looks of it. She says:

"What is your name, dear?"

"Teresa Wignall."

"How old are you?"

"I'm nine."

"And are you new?"

"Yes, Miss."

"Have you moved from another school?"

112

A pause. The child hestitates. Then:

"I've only just come . . ."

"Oh, I see. You're new to the area, are you, dear? Have you just moved here?"

"Yes, Miss."

Mrs Pike sighs. She thinks: why does nobody tell me anything? Here is a completely new child and I haven't had any particulars, no address, no phone number. Nothing. And fine parents she must have, not even coming in with their child on the very first day at a new school. Mrs Pike has views about parents. Some parents at any rate. She says, quite kindly, "Could I have your address, please?"

The child bites her lip and looks desperately round the classroom. She looks almost as though she has forgotten, but "24 Anscoat Avenue," she says at last.

"Anscoat Avenue," Mrs Pike repeats. "I'm afraid I don't know it. Are you sure it's not your old address? Where you used to live?"

"Yes, Miss."

"Is it quite neat?"

"Yes, Miss."

"And will you be staying for dinner or going home?"

"I don't know, Miss."

"Well have you brought dinner money?"

"No, Miss."

"Then perhaps you'd better go home, just for today and see what your mother says," Mrs Pike smiles. Why is the child looking so terrified? Perhaps she's frightened of going home? Mrs Pike adds: "Or you could stay, if you like, just for today. It may be a little far for you to go on your own. We'll sort out the money another day. Right, Teresa, go back to your desk. Wendy, will you and Susan look after Teresa today please, and see that she knows what to do, and where to go?"

*

113

"Will you read, Teresa, please, from the top of page five?"

Teresa bends her head. She has tears in her eyes. She whispers to Wendy: "I can't. I don't know how . . ."

"Shh. I'll help you. Listen to me." Wendy is a good reader. She mutters the words under her breath and Teresa repeats them slowly. Her voice falters.

"Please, Miss!" Nick puts his hand up.

"Yes, Nick?" Miss Pike frowns at him.

"Please, Miss, Wendy was helping her. I heard. She was telling her the words."

"That's no concern of yours, Nick," says Mrs Pike calmly. "Carry on reading from where Teresa left off, please."

Mrs Pike looks at Teresa while Nick is reading. She sits quite upright in her desk. The sunlight shines through the skin of her hands so that she seems almost transparent. I shall have to see what school she came from. Mrs Pike thinks. Not a very good one, that's certain. She looks intelligent enough, but it's clear she can't read. As Nick sits down, Mrs Pike puts R. R. next to Teresa's name on the register. Remedial Reading.

Nobody in Junior Two takes much notice of Samantha. She is quiet, ordinary-looking, not specially clever nor specially stupid. She is sitting in the desk beside Teresa Wignall, thinking, wondering whether or not she is feeling quite well. She feels cold. She didn't feel like that before she sat down. Walking over to the book corner to fetch a book was like stepping into a warm bath. Almost as soon as she left her desk she felt all right again, but the cold air washed over her as she sat down.

"Are you cold? Can you feel a draught?" she asks her neighbour, Mary.

"No, not really," Mary isn't interested.

Samantha feels dizzy, mad, peculiar, but she is sure the cold is coming from Teresa. How can that be? She turns to look at the new girl, sitting silently with her hands folded in her lap. Impulsively, she puts a hand out as if to touch her, then draws it back, frightened. The air around Teresa is burning cold. Touching it is like having fingers on a block of solid ice.

At playtime, Wendy pulls Nick's hair for telling tales. Nick kicks Wendy and the teacher on duty in the playground sends them to stand outside the staffroom door until lessons begin.

Wendy says: 'Sh, they're talking about Teresa in there. Let's listen."

"Who cares about stupid old Teresa?" Nick is sulky. It's not his idea of playtime, milling about outside the staffroom door. Wendy comes close to the door to listen. The Headmaster has a carrying voice. Bits of what he's saying creep through to Wendy and she puts them together, like a jigsaw.

"Never heard of her . . . no new children in Junior Two that I know of . . . Wignall . . . Anscoat Avenue . . . I don't know . . . write to the Education Authority of course . . . got to have come from somewhere . . . there'd be a record if she's just moved here from another part of the country . . . Anscoat Avenue, isn't that one of the little streets behind the White Lion?. . . Rings a bell . . . Remedial Reading, you say?. . . Better give her Free Dinners till we find out more about her . . . sounds like a case of neglect . . . I don't know . . . I honestly don't know how parents expect us to do the lot singlehanded."

Samantha watches Teresa as the children form a line to walk to the canteen. The cold feeling has gone.

115

Perhaps, thinks Samantha, it is because we're out-side, but now there is a mistiness around Teresa's head.

"Can you see a kind of mist around Teresa's head?" Samanatha asks Julie.

"You need your eyes looking at," says Julie and turns to talk to someone else.

Maybe I do, Samantha thinks. Maybe the mist is in my eyes. But she knows it isn't.

Afternoon playtime Teresa is standing with Wendy and Susan in a patch of sunlight by the graveyard wall.

"I like your dress," Wendy says. "I wish my mum would let me wear my long dress to school."

"I would like a dress like yours," Teresa says. She speaks so quietly that the others have to bend their heads to hear her.

"I would like . . ." she begins, then shakes her head.

"What?" Susan says.

"My mother is dead," Teresa says suddenly. Wendy is the first to speak, after the silence.

"Who do you live with, then? Your father? Have you got any brothers or sisters?"

"No," Teresa shakes her head. "Not any more."

The girls are going to ask more questions, but the bell goes. The next lesson is P.E.

Mrs Pike comes prepared. She has found an old leotard in the Lost Property cupboard, and some shabby pumps. She tries to hand them to Teresa discreetly, so as not to embarrass the child, but everyone notices and a whisper goes round the cloakroom:

"Teresa Wignall's not got any P.E. things of her own."

"Must be dead poor."

116

"Bit weird, if you ask me."
"It's not her fault. She can't help it."
"Must be daft, not bringing P.E. stuff."

A surprise! Teresa can float over the highest boxes with no effort at all. She can balance on the narrowest bar of all, she seems almost to be weightless. Mrs Pike is delighted and lavish with her praise. Even the boys are silenced. By the end of the lesson, Nick has put forward a theory that Teresa is a runaway from a travelling circus. Well, it would fit the facts, wouldn't it? Funny clothes, no money, can't read . . . it fits. It does.

Samantha's mother is always one of the last to get to the playground. Samantha has often asked to go home by herself, or with a friend, and the answer is always the same: "When you're ten, dear." So Samantha waits by the railings quite patiently. She likes looking at everyone else's mums. There's Teresa, she thinks, but where's her mother? There are no grown-ups anywhere near her. Perhaps she's allowed to walk home alone . . . lucky thing. Samantha watches her walking out of the gate. The mistiness is still clinging to her outline. Then she's gone. Samantha waits and then becomes aware of someone watching her from the churchyard. She turns and is just in time to see a flash of pale hair ducking down behind the wall. Silly, she thinks, it could be anyone. But she knows it isn't. She knows who it is. Teresa. There's something very strange about Teresa. Samantha is frightened of her. But, she thinks, I wish I knew what I was frightened of. Exactly what it was.

Wendy and Susan walk home together. Wendy's mum fetches them both.

"Did you see where Teresa went?" says Susan.

"No, I didn't. One minute she was there in the cloakroom and the next minute she was gone."

"Must look tomorrow. I want to see if anyone fetches her. Probably one of the Orphanage people." Susan looks knowing. She and Wendy and Liz have decided that Teresa lives in an orphanage. Nick's circus theory is O.K. but, as Liz puts it. "She's got to live somewhere now, hasn't she? Even if she has run away."

From:
Headmaster
St Peter's School
Wallington
5 September 1983

To: Chief Education Officer
Sceptre House
Wordsworth Crescent

Dear Sir

I am writing to ask whether you have any record of a Teresa Wignall, aged 9, of 24 Anscoat Avenue, Wallington. She has arrived in my school with no documentation whatsoever and I would be grateful for any particulars that you can give me about her previous background.

Yours faithfully,
Frank Swithin.

Tomorrow. Tomorrow I will have to tell them. I will tell Wendy and Susan. They will be frightened. Will they still talk to me? But I must tell them. Otherwise they will ask and ask, question after question and I shan't be able to answer. I am going to learn to read. All by myself with Miss Harris. I can tell the letters. I can remember them, after all this time. I can make them with a pencil.

118

And I can read some words. Soon I will be able to read whole stories. I know the numbers. I can add them together a little. I will learn so much. And they will help me to learn. Not Mrs Pike. Mrs Pike wouldn't believe me. Wouldn't believe in me. And then how could I stay?

Wendy, Susan and Teresa are sitting in a corner of the cloakroom, half-hidden by coats. The others have gone out to play. Susan is crying quietly. She has shrunk away a little from Teresa and Wendy. Wendy is trembling all over, but she manages to speak.

"If you are . . . what you say you are, then prove it. Or we won't believe you. Go on. Prove it. Go through that wall. Then we'll know you're not fibbing."

"Are you sure you want me to?" Teresa whispers.

"Yes."

"And you, Susan?"

"Stop snivelling, Susan, or she'll never show us," Wendy says.

Teresa walks over to the wall and disappears.

Then she slides out from between the basins, seeping out of the wall like a transparent formless mist that gradually takes on Teresa's shape and then thickens, becomes a person.

"It's like colouring in a drawing!" Susan squeals. "At first you were just an outline and then you sort of filled yourself in. Please do it again."

Teresa shakes her head. "No, I daren't. I want . . . I want to be like you. I would like you to be my friends. Will you tell the others? They'll be frightened. You were frightened at first. But please don't tell anyone else . . . in another class, or in your families . . . Please."

"O.K." says Wendy. "We won't, will we?" She glares round at Susan.

"Of course we won't, silly. But will you tell us things?" Susan wants to know. "Like what it's like to be a ghost? Do you sleep and eat and that? Do you

119

talk to other ghosts? Do you haunt people? Will you tell us, Teresa, please."

"It's long," Teresa says. "It's long and weary. You watch the seasons turning and know that it's forever. It's very long . . . I've seen so many children from over the wall. It's a long time till you have the courage to join in. I hear the songs and the stories from the other side of the wall. I want to learn. I want to play. That's all."

The bell goes. Junior Two bustle into the classroom. Wendy and Susan link arms with Teresa. They carry Teresa's secret clutched tight within them: something precious, something rare. Time enough to tell the others later on.

From: Chief Education Officer
Sceptre House
Wordsworth Crescent
12 September 1983

To: Frank Swithin, M.A.
St Peter's School
Wallington

Dear Sir
With reference to your letter about Teresa Wignall, I have to inform you that I am unable to find a record of this child. I am, however, making further enquiries, and will let you know as soon as I have any information at all.

Yours faithfully,
Horace Underhill.

Frank Swithin, Headmaster, snorts loudly. The tip of his nose has turned purple—a sign of rage.

"Bloody incompetents at Sceptre House!' he bellows. "Not a blind bit of use at all." He sighs, shakes his head and coughs. The tip of his nose subsides to a pale shade of mauve. He mutters to Mrs Pike:

"Never mind, dear Mrs Pike. I'm sure you're doing a grand job. Any child that turns up in this school is to be taught. Am I right? Or am I wrong?"

"Absolutely right, Mr Swithin," Mrs Pike says quietly. "Absolutely."

"Good, good," says Mr Swithin. The tip of his nose is pink once more. Quite normal.

The days go by. Junior Two is a class with a ghost in it. The children have become accustomed to the thought. At first, of course, it was different. Samantha fainted when she heard. Julie had hysterics and had to be taken home. Nick and Kevin wanted to tell everyone: newspapers, teachers, television, the whole world, but Wendy had told them what would happen if they did: they would be haunted all their lives by the very horriblest ghosts in the universe. Teresa had said so, Wendy whispered. It wasn't true. Teresa had said nothing of the kind, but it worked. Nick and Kevin were silent. Dinners were a problem at first, because Teresa could not eat, but all the children helped. One speared up the meat and ate it while the dinner lady's back was turned, another slid the vegetables off Teresa's plate, and Samantha (who ate everything that other people hated, like rice pudding and sago and stewed gooseberries and lumpy custard) generally dealt with the afters.

One day each member of the class was given a small envelope and told to collect as much money as they could for the blind.

"We'll each bring two pence extra," Susan had announced, "and put it in Teresa's envelope."

At the end of the week, Teresa had fifty-eight pence and Mrs Pike was very pleased. She hadn't expected half that sum.

"What a lot of money, dear," she said. "Well done."

"My friends helped me." Teresa said.

"That's what friends are for, aren't they, dear? And it's such a good cause."

The days go by. Junior Two is a class with a ghost in it. The children don't mind at all.

A class with a ghost in it. Sometimes, at playtime, Mrs Pike's children congregate beside the bicycle shed to watch Teresa disappear through the wall and reappear again. Three children keep watch, make sure that no one is looking. Nick asks Teresa to float right over the wall: up and over like a bird, and Teresa does to. Everyone claps. Teresa enjoys the applause, the admiration, being someone special . . .

A class with a ghost in it. The children are making little linen mats, embroidering them with coloured silks. Teresa threads the needle right through her hand, as though it weren't there at all, and feels nothing. Wendy and Liz think this is very impressive.

"Do it again," they whisper.

"No, don't," says Susan. "It's horrid. It makes me feel sick to look."

"Then don't look," says Wendy. "Turn your back to us. Baby!"

Teresa does it again, just to oblige her friends.

A class with a ghost in it. Mrs Pike calls Teresa to her desk.

"How are you getting on, dear? I hear good things about you from Miss Harris. She says you're reading very well now. Are you enjoying school?"

"Oh, yes, Miss," Teresa nods vigorously.

"There's just one thing," Mrs Pike frowns. "I would like to see your mother, dear. Do you think you could ask her to come and see me one day?" Mrs Pike is thinking: How can anyone let their child wear the same clothes, day in, day out? Mrs Pike refused to believe that anyone can be so poor or so neglectful. Teresa hangs her head. Mrs Pike persists.

"Will you, dear? Will you ask her to come and see me? I'd like to meet her. And I'd like to tell her how well you're getting on."

"She can't come," Teresa says suddenly. "She's ill. In hospital."

Mrs Pike says: "Oh dear. Poor thing. Will she be there long? Who is looking after you? Is it your father? Perhaps he could come?"

"He's dead."

"Oh, goodness, I am sorry," Mrs Pike is confused. This is a matter for the Head. But . . .

"You must be looked after by somebody . . ."

"My auntie," says Teresa after a pause. "But she couldn't come in. She's ever so busy. She's got a new baby. I don't think she'll come in."

"Very well, dear," Mrs Pike sighs. "Go back and finish your sums."

She thinks to herself: this is a case for the Social Security if ever I saw one. I shall go round there tomorrow night and speak to the aunt. It shouldn't be allowed, such a nice little girl, so quiet and such a hard worker—and the children all seem to like her and be protective of her. Mrs Pike makes a note on her memo pad: look up Anscoat Avenue in the *A to Z*.

Two days later, Mrs Pike and Mr Swithin have a serious talk about Teresa.

"I went myself, in the end," says Mrs Pike. "I found Anscoat Avenue. I found number 24. It's a Chinese takeaway. No one there had ever heard of Teresa Wignall. I tried number 42. And number 2. And 4. No one had heard of her." Poor Mrs Pike is at a loss. Worried. "She must live somewhere. She's a truthful child. I'm sure. Why would she say Anscoat Avenue if that isn't where she lives?"

Mr Swithin grunts. "I'll write to the Education office again. Chivvy them up a bit. Don't you worry about it, Mrs Pike. You're doing a grand job with the child. She's coming on splendidly."

Junior Two is a class with a ghost in it. A ghost who is coming on splendidly.

Miss Harris feels pleased. This Teresa Wignall has made good progress. Learned such a lot. She read well now. A little slowly, but well. It is a sunny afternoon in October. Outside, the air has some of the sharpness of autumn in it, but in the classroom you could imagine it was summer still. It's a Friday. The end of a long week. Teresa is reading aloud, but Miss Harris is tired. The warmth has made her drowsy. She is thinking of tonight. Tonight she will put on her red jersey dress and go out to dinner with her fiancé and they will talk. Teresa has a soft voice. It melts into the warmth of the classroom, almost lulling Miss Harris to sleep:

"The witch pushed Gretel up close to the oven. The fire was roaring and spitting, burning with flames that leapt and jumped out of the door, nearly scorching her dress. 'Look in, my dear,' said the witch, 'to see if it's properly heated, and then we'll bake the bread.'

'I don't know how to,' said Gretel. 'Will you show me, please?'

'It's easy,' said the witch. 'Look, I'll show you.' She stood by her side, and as she bent towards the flames, Gretel pushed her right in the fire, shut the iron door and locked her in with the flames . . .' Teresa's voice fades to nothing. Miss Morris is roused suddenly by the silence. "We'll have to stop now. but you can keep

124

the book for the weekend if you like." She gathers her papers together. Stands up.

"No, thank you, Miss," says Teresa. She is shaking, nearly in tears.

"It's a horrible book. I hate it."

"But it ends happily, dear. Really it does. That's the wicked witch you know, who was going to eat Hansel. She deserves it, doesn't she?"

"Nobody deserves it," Teresa whispers. "Nobody. Nobody deserves that."

Miss Harris sighs. "Perhaps you're right. It is rather gruesome. Never mind, we'll find a happy story next week."

Teresa slips from the room. Miss Harris is already thinking of what she will tell her fiancé: "Imagine it, Neil. A child in this day and age, with all that violence on television, who trembles at Hansel and Gretel. I've noticed, of course, that she is a sensitive child."

I remember now. That story reminded me. I remember fire. Paint bubbling on the windowsills, paper curling into long black rolls, the bannisters lit up with bars of shining white and yellow. And the smoke. Filling my mouth like water, filling my eyes and burning them and choking me, a fog everywhere. Everywhere. Nowhere that wasn't a fog, a sooty, smelly blanket over everything. The smell of things scorching. And sounds. Tearing and crashing and the roar of the flames, and over everything else, screaming. I remember it all now. I know how I died. But the others—did they die too? There's none of them buried here. I know that.

George Macmahon is sweeping leaves, marvelling as he does every year that such quantities of them should land in his playground from trees that don't look more than ordinarily leafy in the summer. The children, of course, make it worse, gathering them into heaps all over the place, spreading them into

125

patterns, kicking them this way and that. He groans. Not long now. A few more weeks, then retirement. Most of the time, George thinks of the idle days that are coming with something like dread, but not on a bitter cold afternoon like this. He turns his mind, deliberately, to gas fires, slippers, hot tea, toast, television . . . nearly done now. On his way to the shed to put away the broom, he catches sight of someone in the graveyard. A child, wandering around.

"Here, you!" he calls. "Aren't you one of our kids?"

The child stops. Looks at him. Nods silently. George turns red with fury. Bloody kids! Never a thought for their parents, most likely worried sick. He shouts at the little girl:

"Get off home now! Go on. Your mam'll be that worried. Go on now, hurry up. The bell went twenty minutes ago. You'll catch your death out here."

The child runs away. George shakes his head. Whatever next? Parents to blame as much as the kids, when you stop to think. What kind of parent wouldn't come and meet a little thing like that on a dark afternoon? Asking for trouble, were some people. Asking for it.

From: Chief Education Officer
Sceptre House
Wordsworth Crescent
3 November 1983

To: Frank Swithin, M.A.
St Peter's School
Wallington

Dear Sir

Further to your recent enquiry. I should like to assure you that we have in no way let the matter drop, as you put it.

126

You are certainly aware of the time such things can take and the care with which we have to check all the facts that become available to us. We have been in touch with ten other Local Authorities in the immediate vicinity with no success. We have found six Teresa Wignalls but all six have been verified as attending other schools.

We could, of course, extend our search to cover the whole country, and will do so if necessary. However, certain facts have come to light which may be of interest to you.

1) 24 Anscoat Avenue is now a Chinese Takeaway shop with a flat above it. This flat is lived in by the proprietors of the afore-mentioned eating place.

2) We have traced the previous owners of the property through local Estate Agents. The house was rebuilt in 1903 after having been destroyed by fire in July of 1902. The householder at the time of the fire was a Mrs Frances Wignall, a mother of five children. One child, Teresa Wignall, aged nine, died in the blaze. There is no further record of this family.

It is only as an interesting coincidence that I draw these facts to your attention. It is, of course, clearly impossible that a child who died some eighty years ago should be attending your school. You may rest assured therefore, that we shall be pursuing our enquiries.

Yours sincerely
Horace Underhill.

Several members of staff feel distinctly faint when Mr Swithin reads out the letter to a hastily assembled Staff Meeting at the end of the afternoon.

Teresa, hiding in the lavatories till everyone else had gone home, hears loud voices coming from the staff room, and listens. Mr Swithin is shouting:

"It's all a lot of nonsense. A mistake. I don't believe in ghosts. Never have and never will, and the idea of having one in my school, mixing with our children is simply monstrous. I will not stand for it and that's that. Mrs Pike, don't cry, please. You will tackle the child in the morning and that'll put an end, once and for all to this ghost rubbish. I've never heard anything like it in my life. There's many a funny letter I've had from the Education Authority in my time, but this beats all, it does really. A ghost in my school! How can rational adults even begin to believe such things?"

Teresa drifts out to the playground, over the wall, back to the graveyard. She looks at the dark windows of the school, her school and wishes she could remember how to cry. She thinks: I can never go there again. Mr Swithin doesn't want me there, mixing with the other children. I'm bad for them. He doesn't believe in me. I can't show myself again. They mustn't see me. They'll get into trouble. Monstrous, that's what he said. Monstrous. I shall see them and they'll never know. I must say goodbye, but how? How?

Junior Two is quiet today. Teresa, Mrs Pike says, trying to look cheerful, will not be coming back. We will all miss her, she says, and there are tears in her eyes. Some of the children are crying.

"Open your reading books, children," says Mrs Pike. Wendy opens her book and finds a small piece of paper tucked between the pages. "Dear Wendy. They have found out about me. I can't come back because Mr Swithin will be cross and not allow it. I will miss you. Please come to the wall and wave because I will be looking for you though you may not be able to see me any more now. Thank you for looking after me. Love to everyone. Teresa."

Wendy bursts into noisy tears and doesn't stop crying till milktime.

Wendy, Susan, Liz, Nick and Kevin stand by the graveyard wall and wave.

128

"D'you think she's there?" Liz asks.

"Of course she is," says Wendy. "She said she would be, didn't she?"

She raises her voice: "Teresa! Hello! Can you see me?"

"Don't be daft, Wendy," says Nick. "What ever do you think you look like, shouting into the air like that?"

"I'm going to shout," says Wendy, "so there, I don't want Teresa to think we've forgotten her."

Christmas comes, and then January. A new term. The children of Junior Two no longer stand and wave by the graveyard wall. The memory of Teresa begins to fade. Occasionally, Wendy will turn and shout over the wall, raise her hand, but even she does so less and less frequently. It's not that Junior Two have forgotten Teresa: only that she is no longer in the very top layer of their minds. Thoughts of her lie in corners of the memory, like dreams from the night before last.

Mr Edgeburton is the new Caretaker. He is stiff and thin and quiet. He has bushy eyebrows. He never smiles. Once upon a time, he was in the Navy. Or the Army, no one knows for sure. He walks very upright, as though on parade. He is not given to gossiping with either the staff or the children. But he keeps the place spick and span, there's no denying it. He is keen on security. He has had locks made for every room in the school, and patrols the corridors every afternoon, locking up. One day, as he is about to turn the key in the Library door, he notices a child reading in the corner. He knows exactly how to deal with the situation. He strides into the room and towers over the small child. "Hello, hello, hello," he says, "what have we here, then? An eager scholar, is it? Come along now, girl, what time do you call this? Get along home this instant, before I lock you in here for the night."

The child looks at him. Stands up and puts the book back on the shelf. "I'm sorry," she whispers as she slides out of the door. "I should think so too! Whatever next? I've heard of playing truant from school, but I've never heard of a child who played truant from home." He almost smiles at his own joke, but the child has gone.

He locks the Library door, and carries on down the corridor, rattling his keys. Feeling important.

> I will go back, Teresa thinks. I will go back after he has gone home, and finish the book. And then I will start another. There are friends in the books. People and children that are only half-real, like me. There is a world inside those pages that someone like me can live in for ever.

Mr Edgeburton, having locked up, is on his way home. Turning back towards the school gates he thinks he sees the half-transparent form of a girl float like a curl of smoke above the playground wall. He rubs his eyes and looks again. Nothing. All the way home, he worries about what it might have been. By the time he opens his front door, he has decided that it was only a sheet of newspaper, borne upwards by the wind.

The Roseline Tape

One, two, three . . . testing, testing. Isn't that what you're supposed to say to a microphone? I don't know if this is the same, though. It's recording my voice, isn't it, and not amplifying it. I can't think why you need what you sometimes call "my feelings" and other times call "my version of events". I mean, isn't this a loony bin? Isn't everyone here crazy, me included? Are the words of a loony to be trusted? I know you hate that word: crazy. You like words like 'disturbed' better, but I don't think I'm disturbed at all. It sounds messy, like a rumpled drawer. I feel quite tidy and well-arranged. In my own crazy way, of course. Are you catching all these words? I can see them as I'm speaking, squashing through the silver mesh at the front of this cassette recorder and coming out the other side as tape, all flat and shiny and brown. There they are, winding themselves round and round on to little black plastic spools. Have you ever seen a mincer? If you put meat in and turn the handle, red and white worms come out. If my words looked like that, all raw and bleeding, I wouldn't be a bit surprised, but it wouldn't half mess up your equipment, tee hee!

It's very quiet here. At the Roseline, it was very noisy. I find all this silence quite strange. You have to understand about the Roseline Hotel or nothing I'm going to tell you will make sense. Do you know the song "Hotel California"? It's one of my best songs ever, about this hotel in the middle of a desert. In this song, it says that you can check out of the Hotel

California any time you like but you can never leave it. The Roseline's just the same. It's with you always. It's with me now. The thing is, it's more than just an ordinary hotel. It's a kingdom. Huge. The biggest hotel on the Island, though not necessarily the best. We can accommodate five hundred people. We have bingo and cabarets every night. We have seven floors of bedrooms. We have the Barbados Bar, the Captain's Cabin Snuggery, the Writing Room, the TV Lounge, the Reception Area, the Poolside Bistro with the top bits of yellow beach umbrellas stuck to the yellow ceiling . . . how sunny and bright it looks even at 2 a.m! We have a dining room that stretches across acres of yellow carpet and in this dining room, waitresses in yellow dresses and white aprons flutter between the tables like small birds. My dad used to wear what he called his penguin suit and watch over the dining room: see that everyone had a table; arrange for this and that and the other to be done . . . he always told me it was a very responsible job, and I suppose it was. Tiring, too, at mealtimes, having to walk about like that, patrolling the strips of carpet between the tables, making sure everything was "tickety-boo". That was an expression my dad liked. "Peachy-creamy" was another. Also "hunky-dory". He'd been to America once. His name was Arthur. He's dead now, but you know that, of course. It was an accident. That's what everyone says. But I'm not telling this in the right order. It's messy. You will have every right to call me disturbed if I carry on like this. Where was I? The Roseline . . . a kingdom. Yes.

Well, Molly is the Queen of the Roseline and she used to be married to the King of the Roseline, Howard. They had . . . they have . . . a son called Seth. Howard's brother, Roger, also works at the Roseline. He used to be in charge of the entertain-

132

ments. Every evening at 8.00 in the Barbados Bar, under the whispering branches of the plastic palm trees, he'd call out the numbers for the bingo . . . clickety click . . . two fat ladies . . . Sherwood Forest . . . key to the door . . . and his silver-spangled jacket would glitter under the coloured lights, and all the guests would squeak and squirm with excitement. Seth and I used to laugh at him. Laugh at the guests, too, I'm afraid. They were always so shiny and pink from the beach: all the ladies so rustly and frothy in their new clothes bought specially for the holiday . . . and Roger used to flirt with them something rotten . . . touch them whenever he could, and make remarks about their figures and play stupid games with them on party nights where they had to pump up balloons hidden in the trousers of their gentlemen friends . . . oh, it was revolting. Roger was revolting. Woe betide any guest who was a bit overweight. He'd make fun of them non-stop. If it had been me, I'd have burst into tears, but the strange thing was, they loved it. They giggled and wriggled, and shrieked with laughter and all their separate chins and rolls of flesh shook and wobbled. Seth and I never stayed in the Barbados Bar for long.

"It's painful," Seth used to say. "*He's* painful." And he would shudder. "How can two brothers be so different? I mean, look at him. Can you believe we're even related?"

That was Before. There's always a Before, isn't there, and an After? Before Howard died is what I mean.

I don't know if I can explain properly what everything was like Before. We were happy, all of us, that was the main thing. There was Howard, so tall and straight and dignified, running things. Managing whole battalions of maids, cooks, waitresses, cleaners, couriers, barmen and seeing to it that all the

133

hundreds of visitors who came to the Roseline all through the year, were happy. The Roseline didn't have an out-of-season time. Not really. We were open all the year round. That's like the Hotel California as well. Any time of year, the songs says, plenty of room at the Hotel California. At Christmas time, instead of the young families with small kids and couples pretending not to be middle-aged, we had the old people from the Mainland looking for somewhere mild to spend the winter. The Island is supposed to be ten degrees warmer than the Mainland. Did you know that? At the Roseline, of course, it's warm all the year round. There is a yellowness about the warmth. It wraps itself around you like blankets. Howard and Molly must have liked yellow as a colour: the whole hotel is decorated in shades of yellow and orange and mustard and brown, but what you think when you walk into it is: YELLOW. Still, as I say, everyone was happy. Howard managed. Molly looked glamorous in Reception and pinning the menus up on the notice-board each day. She's yellow too. Have you seen her? Yellow hair, up in a French pleat, and golden skin and gold chains and bracelets and a love of tight, shiny dresses. "To show off my assets," she used to say to me, winking down at the breasts that swelled like melons under her slippery clothes. Of course you've met her. She must have been the one who brought me here. She likes me. I think she thinks that as I haven't got a mother, she's a sort of substitute. She used to say: "I wish I had a daughter like you," and then she'd sigh. "Boys," she said, "can be so difficult. Look at my darling Seth," she'd say and push her eyebrows up as far as they'd go. And Seth *was* her darling, there's no doubt about that at all. I thought all the kissing and cheek-pinching that went on was a bit much, to tell you the truth, but it flattered and amused Molly when people

134

round the Island mistook them for boyfriend and girlfriend. They used to stroll round the shops hand in hand, and whenever they had a meal at a restaurant, Molly used to feed him little bites from her plate . . . oh, they were very close. Very close indeed. Still, I never thought Seth would react in the strange way that he did . . . but I haven't got there yet, have I? I'm getting ahead of myself. Anyway, I was attached to my father, too, but there certainly wasn't anything flirtatious about our feelings towards one another. Looking back, I think I probably loved my father to protect him from the fact that no one else did, as far as I could make out. Derek, my brother, could hardly spend an hour in his company without showing some kind of irritation . . . grinding his teeth, or shredding the edge of a paper napkin. But I loved my dad. I wish I'd told him that more often, but it's too late now, of course.

Molly was the first to have some idea of me and Seth getting together. Carrying on the Roseline dynasty. She used to give me things. Bits of jewellery and scarves and half-empty bottles of perfume. She'd sit me down in front of her mirror and show me how to put on make-up and how to twist my scarves like this and like that . . . I hated that mirror. It had two wings, one on each side, and when you looked into it you could see hundreds of different views of yourself, all sorts of unexpected images. I felt "disturbed" in front of that mirror, I can tell you, as if I'd been broken into lots and lots of tiny splinters and would never get back together again. And none of it helped either, I'd watch what Molly did to my face with blusher and lip gloss, but when I tried to do it, later in my own room, I looked like a freak from a funfair, and I'd run to the bathroom and wash it all off. Looking at me, Molly would sigh sometimes and shake her head. "Colour, lovey," she'd say, "that's what life is all about . . . colour. You're such a pale, quiet little thing . . ." and her voice would trail off into silence. I knew what she meant, though. She meant: how would I ever get a man, without all the colour and shine that men seemed to like? More particularly, how would I ever catch Seth's eye? It was a question I had been asking myself ever since I could remember. You have to understand something, little recording machine, something very important. I have loved Seth all my life. That's not so strange, is it? It's quite predictable. We grew up together. He is two years older than me. He is my own brother's best friend. We have roamed the corridors of the Roseline Hotel together since we were toddlers stealing sugar-lumps from the breakfast tables before the guests came down. No one did anything to discourage our friendship. Why should they? OK, he was the boss's son and I was only the dining room supervisor's daughter, but no one seemed to mind. Anyway, for years and years everything was fine. And then my brother Derek and Seth and I grew up. I noticed that Derek and Seth, during the summer holidays, seemed to be spending more and more hours at the edge of the swimming pool.

I have avoided mentioning the swimming pool for all this time—have you noticed? Is that significant, do you think? The swimming pool is the glory of the Roseline. It's irregularly-shaped, like two adjoining circles pushed out of true. There's a pale yellow paved area around it. There are deck chairs, and white tables with huge, yellow and white striped beach umbrellas stuck into their centres. Then there's a high wall round the pool, with climbing plants growing all over it . . . rambling roses, and wisteria and jasmine. There are also stone tubs dotted about here and there with flowers growing in them. At the edge of the pool there's an ice-cream and soft drinks kiosk.

I have worked in this kiosk every summer since I was thirteen, and that's how it came about that I had such a good view of what Derek and Seth were doing. My dad called it "cavorting". This "cavorting" involved a lot of laughter with young girls in bikinis; a lot of rubbing in of suntan lotion on backs and thighs and stomachs (let's see how near we can get to a breast, snigger, snigger); a lot of pretend-fighting and splashing in the water that allowed them to try and catch hold of the oily bodies, and that sometimes resulted in a bikini-top coming adrift . . . then there would be shrieks of pretend-horror, and little plump breasts like apples would bob about in the blue, and hands would touch them accidentally-on-purpose, and then the shrieking would start again, and then the girls would struggle out of the pool, all glistening like seals, and Seth and Derek would help to dry them off in yellow, fluffy Roseline hotel towels, and then the oiling would begin again.

"Frolicking". . . that was another word my dad used. Also "gambolling". I just put scoop after scoop of pastel ice-cream into yellow wafer cones and felt as though my heart was being shredded. Do you know the way Kleenex tears raggedly and softly when you pull at it? That's what I felt like as I looked at Seth. Torn and soft and ready to crumple myself up and throw myself away. But I smiled at the children and doled out the ice-cream and no one ever knew. Not Molly. Not Derek, and certainly not Seth. Oh, no. Seth thought we were just as we'd been from the day we were born: good mates. We still had long chats together, we still giggled together at Ropey Roger doing the bingo whenever Seth managed to tear himself away from the pool and the lure of all that soft, greased flesh turning golden in the sun. But we weren't the same. Not a bit the same. Something had changed, and that was me. I was different. I didn't look different. I was still thin, and dark and pale, and I'd given up hope of ever having breasts like melons, but I was different inside. And because I was different inside, I wanted Seth to be different in the way he treated me. There was one special day when I noticed this. I'd always been jealous watching Seth and Derek enjoying themselves at the pool, because I wanted them not to forget my existence. I wanted to be included in the general fun and games ... the "larks" my dad called them. Anyway, on this particular day, I was just taking some money from a little kid, and as I gave her back the change, I saw that Seth and one of the oily girls were far away from all the laughing, splashing others, right down in the shallow end with all the babies, practically under my nose. As I watched, I saw Seth push a curtain of hair away from this girl's face, and I saw his mouth being swallowed by her mouth, and then I saw their bodies stretched out in the shallow water ... stuck together, and I felt as if my insides had turned to ice. I ran out of the kiosk and into the loo and then I was sick. I wasn't sick because I was disgusted, I was sick, I realized afterwards as I sat in the loo, shaking with cold and pain, because *I* wanted that: I wanted Seth's mouth fastened on to my mouth, and his body pressed against mine, and his hands rubbing fragrant oils into my skin. I was weak, sick with wanting it. That was when I knew that my love for Seth was different: different from what it had always been and different from anything I would ever feel for anyone else ever again. I could have asked to be moved from the kiosk. I could have gone and looked after the babies in the crèche, and I wouldn't have needed to look at him, but I couldn't help it. I needed to see him, whatever he was doing. I wanted to look at the blue water and the deckchairs and the flowers growing up the wall. Sometimes Seth and the oily girls weren't there. I knew where they were. Once I had such a strong image of what they must be doing that I dropped four full double-choc cornets on the floor and burst into tears. Molly came and took me into her private sitting room and gave me a cup of tea. I pretended I was having my period, and she gave me some pills.

The thing about the oily girls was, they left after a couple of weeks. This one must have been special, though, because when she left, Seth went into one of his sulks. He often went into sulks. He stopped cavorting and frolicking and took to reading on his bed for hours without saying a word. I used to go in and sit with him sometimes.

"It's my A levels next year," he said, when I asked him why he was doing so much reading. "And then I'm off."

"Off?" I said.

"To the Mainland. To university."

I must have looked as sad as I felt, because he said, "It's not the end of the world, you know. There's still the holidays."

"But how will I live if you're not here?" I asked, and something in my voice must have struck him strangely, because he put his book down and looked at me. Looked right into me. He has these very pale grey eyes that seem to look inside a person . . . do you know what I mean?

"Won't you be happy?" he asked.

"I'll die."

"Don't die. I'd hate it if you died."

"Why?"

"What do you mean, why?" he asked. "Because . . . because . . ."

"You can't say it," I said. "I can say it. It's easy. Look at me saying it. I love you." I sat down on his bed, near his feet. He sat up at once and giggled. Then he said:

139

"And I love you too. There you are. I've said it."

"But you don't mean it. You have to mean it."

"I *do* mean it. I can't think of anyone except my mum and dad that I love better than you."

"I don't mean that."

"Like what?"

"Like a sister or something."

"What *do* you mean then?" He'd sat up by now. He started stroking his finger along the underside of my arm, very gently. I thought: my skin will blister and burn where he's touched it.

"I mean," I stammered, "I saw you. In the pool. Kissing that girl."

"And what did you feel?"

I turned my head away so that he shouldn't see me. The words didn't seem to be able to get past my throat. Seth said again: "What did you feel?" Only by now, his mouth was near my ear, he was whispering into my ear, so that I could feel his breath. "Did you want it to be you that I was kissing? Yes? Did you?"

Oh, his breathing, his breathing and his voice blowing through my hair! I was becoming a volcano. I turned to him, and my mouth found his mouth, and although I'd never kissed anyone in my life before, I suddenly knew exactly how to do it, and all the feelings I'd had and all the love I'd felt came rushing out of me, covering me and Seth with white fire.

Much later, hours later, we went down to the pool to swim. We didn't cavort, or frolic or gambol, but we held hands and floated together in the turquoise water, and when our bodies drifted into one another, our swollen mouths would meet in a kiss that tasted of chlorine. When we got out, Seth wrapped me in a fluffy yellow towel, as if I were a baby. That was last year, in September. September 6th, to be precise, I wrote it in my diary. I could show it to you. It says: "Seth loves me. He said so." He did say it. That

140

afternoon and many times after that. He says now he didn't, but he did. He's so different now. I wrote it down, you see, so that there should be no mistake. But I can see that you might be a bit doubtful. I'm here, aren't I? On the funny farm, isn't it a bit suspicious that I can remember every word of a conversation like that? Didn't it sound a bit like a play I'd made up and memorised? I don't care, little machine. I don't care what you think, because *I* know, I know.

We were a couple after that. A pair. Everyone knew it. Molly remarked that I'd found a better complexion-improver than blusher and giggled. She can be a bit crude sometimes. Ropey Roger made jokes about us in the Barbados Bar. The young Prince of the Roseline and his lovely Princess, he'd croon into the mike, and all the ladies hearts would flutter looking at Seth. I was happy. He was mine for nearly a year and then he went to university on the Mainland, and the whole world looked as though someone had switched the light off. That was Before. Then Howard died. Food poisoning, they said. One day he was fine and the next day he was dead. The Roseline went into mourning. Seth came to the funeral and then had to go straight back.

"I'll see you at Christmas, he said, holding both my hands at the airport, saying goodbye. "Everything will be better. You'll see."

But everything wasn't better. It was worse. Molly married Roger less than eight weeks after Howard's death. Some gossips said she must have been carrying on with Roger even while Howard was alive, but she hadn't.

"I don't know," she said to me once as she was getting made-up for Talent Night in the Barbados Bar, "why everyone has to be so unkind. I'm just the sort of person who *needs* a husband. I'd be quite lost

141

without one. *You* know what I mean." And she winked at me in the glass, woman to woman. I didn't know what she meant. I still don't. The idea of anyone else at all in all the world touching me in the way Seth does . . . the way Seth did . . . makes me want to vomit. As for Roger, I can't even feel sick. The thought paralyses me.

When Seth came back at Christmas and found them married, he changed completely. If I say, he went mad, you'll think I'm exaggerating. I'm not. He stomped around the place, being sullen. Rude to guests. Rude to Roger, and cold, cold, cold to me.

I asked him straight out in the Barbados Bar one night. A band was playing, so we had to speak loudly to be heard. I said:

"What's the matter, Seth? Can't you tell me? Don't you love me any more? Don't you remember how we were?"

"No," he said. "We weren't ever anything. You're imagining it. All you bloody women," he shouted at me and his eyes blazed, "you're all the bloody same. All you care about is sex. That's all you're interested in. Sex, sex, sex! I don't care if I never touch another woman ever again."

I left then, and went to my room. I felt as if I were in a coffin and the lid had closed on top of me. I felt suffocated.

I tried at first to make all sorts of excuses for him. His father dying—that was sad. His mother marrying someone he hated . . . that was enough to make a person miserable. And maybe there *was* something (just a teeny, weeny something) *more* about his feelings towards Molly that made him start behaving like her lover, because that's what he did. I can remember feeling, as well as the rawness and pain of being rejected by Seth, little stings of jealousy that he should be so concerned about his mother, and have

142

so little interest in me. I'll give him time, I thought. He'll be better once he gets over all that.

Then, the row happened. Molly had summoned him to her room, probably to tell him off for the way he was carrying on. I think he must have been drinking. That was why, the police said, he had failed to notice my father in the drive as he roared out of the Roseline in Molly's car. I imagine my father, hit by that weight of metal in the dark, and I see his body spiralling up into the night, and coming down slowly, from high, high up, but I know it wasn't like that. They said the impact pushed him to the side of road where he died of a heart attack. One of the barmen found him hours later, lying in a bed of wallflowers. Oh, Dad, I can't bear to think of you lying there all alone! I can't bear to think of all the things you might have been thinking as the hours passed. I try to think of you not knowing anything about what happened, and that makes me feel a little better.

Afterwards, Molly said Seth'd screamed and shrieked at her. I heard her telling the police. "As if he were jealous," she said. "Can you believe it? As if he were a lover of mine and not my son . . . as if he'd become my husband . . . oh, it was grotesque. He kept on and on about the photos. Made me look at a photo of Howard, then at one of Roger . . . 'How could you leave this for this?' And then he shouted at me. Said he thought I was too old for . . . well you know . . . all that side of things. They're so arrogant, the young, that's the trouble. Think they know it all. Anyway, he stormed out of here saying he was never coming back and (tears here and gulps of anguish) you know the rest. Poor Arthur!"

I can't get used to my old dad being dead. OK, I know he was a bit pompous. I know he was a bit of a bore who used funny words and behaved as though seeing five hundred people in to dinner were the same

143

as organising the Battle of Waterloo, but still. He was my dad. I don't know what Derek will say when he comes back. He took a job on the Mainland last year, but he'll come back now. Not just for Dad but for me. To see what's happened to me.

Nothing's happened to me, though. That's the point. People thought I'd been drinking that night, but I hadn't. Some said the grief had gone to my head. I don't remember much about it. I remember going to the pool and picking all the flowers I could find. I remember vaguely coming into the Barbados Bar and handing flowers to everyone ... I know I gave some to Molly. And to other people. I suppose I must have looked drunk. I suppose that was why they came after me later. I can remember thinking this: how lovely to lie in the black water of the pool and float and drift and pretend that it's still summer. I thought: if I close my eyes, I can pretend that it's still summer. I thought: if I close my eyes, I can pretend that the water is blue. My whole head will fill up with blue and summer and warmth. It will fill me, this blue water, like love. I will be filled with love. Death never really occurred to me. I only wanted to close my eyes and for everything to be blue again.

Molly found me, I think. She brought me here. I have had a visit from Derek. He says Seth should be locked up. He (Seth) is spreading stories in the town about how Ropey Roger (only he's calling him Randy Roger now) was the one who put poison in Howard's food and killed him. Derek says Seth talks wildly all the time. Of course, he has never been to see me. He doesn't love me any more. If he ever did.

It's pretty here. Lovely gardens. There's a brook over there. I can just see it from the window. When I've finished this recording, I think I'll go for a walk and look at it. I can see a willow bending into the water . . . how pretty it is! Someone ought to have a picnic on the bank. An imaginary picnic, perhaps. I'll pretend Seth is with me. I'll pretend we've just been married and he's crowned my head with posies of flowers and put garlands of bright leaves around my neck. I'll pretend I'm wearing a long, silk dress the colour of tea roses, and I'll pretend Seth loves me. I'll be down there soon, soon, little machine. Watch out for me. I'll be so happy, you'll hear me singing. By the stream. Over there. Under the willow branches.

Billy's Hand

I don't know what you've heard about Billy's hand.
Everyone in the class has been so busy inventing,
embroidering, twisting and magnifying what really
happened that it's difficult to sort out the truth. Julia
thinks, for instance, that it was a sort of collective
waking nightmare brought on by the cheese in our
sandwiches: I ask you! So that's what I've decided to
do: tell you exactly what happened, exactly as I
remember it. And I do remember it—after all, wasn't
it me that Billy called for in that horrible moment?
Miss Peters was there too, of course, but she's not
going to give you an account of the events of that
day, you can bet your boots on that. "Hysteria," she
was muttering in the ambulance afterwards. "An
illusion induced by hysteria." I don't know about
that. I thought an illusion was something you saw
that turned out to be not there at all, and you can't
say that about Billy's hand, not really. But I'm
jumping ahead. I mustn't do that. Back to the
beginning.

Billy's hand. Doesn't it just sound like something
from a horror movie? Could it be severed and dripping with blood? I'm sorry if this is a disappointment
to anyone, but there are no severed heads, vampires,
ghosts of the chain-rattling variety, headless horses
or haunted graveyards in this story, no matter what
Sharon and Tracy may have told you. What you're
going to hear may be more or less terrifying, I don't
know, but I can say quite truthfully that I'd rather
meet a couple of thirsty vampires any day than go

through that again, perhaps because vampires, etc. have become quite cosy now that we see them on TV such a lot.

There's another reason why I should be the one to tell the story and that's because I'm Billy's cousin. I'm not only his cousin but I live next door to him and have done all my life. And there's something else: I'm probably the only person in the world (apart from his parents) who likes Billy. The truth is, he's awful. He's a bully, the worst sort of bully, nasty and thoughtful about his unkindness, as if he spends a great deal of time working out just the right torment for the person he's getting at. I know what they say about bullies, that they're all cowards at heart and that you only have to stick up for yourself and they'll run away. Well, our Billy's not like that. He's completely fearless. Or he was completely fearless, I should say. Before that school trip, there wasn't a person on earth he wouldn't have fought, and no one he would have feared to tease or terrify, not even kids with big brothers who threatened to have him beaten up after school, or those with dads who would report him to the Head as soon as look at him.

So why do I like him? Even love him a bit, perhaps. Well, firstly, as the vampires would say, blood is thicker than water. All my life he's been there like a big brother, and no amount of remembering the gouged-out eyes of my favourite dolls, or those dreadful frogs he used to put in my bed because they were my special terror, can change that. He could always run faster, climb higher, and shout louder than me, and so he gave me something to aim for, something to copy. Secondly, he became bored of bullying me by the time we were five. We went to school together (we've been in the same class all along) and there, spread out for his pleasure, were dozens and dozens of new victims, all fresh and ready with huge buckets

147

of tears still waiting to be shed. I learned never to cry years ago. Thirdly, when we moved up into secondary school, he became a kind of protector, sheltering me from the lesser bullies of the class. "Don't touch Kim Harrison," they used to say, "or that Billy'll get you, good and solid. She's his cousin or something." And I was grateful for this protection, and did his homework for him most nights. I also made him promise to lay off all my best friends, but sometimes he forgot. He's not very bright, except at his bullying, you see, but at that he's fiendishly clever. One day, he cut off Shirley's thick, long plait of golden hair in the middle of a film we were watching in the school hall. It was a film about deserts, and suddenly Shirley shrieked and all the lights went on, and there was the cut-off plait under her chair, all lumpy and lifeless and horrid. I looked for Billy, but he was on the other side of the room. I'll never know how he moved so fast, nor what he did with the scissors. The Head never found out who had done it. There was no proof, though I bet he had his suspicions. Shirley cried and cried for hours all through dinner, even though it was sausages, which were her very best food of all. I screamed at Billy all the way home:

"You monster! How could you do it? I *told* you to leave Shirley alone. How could you? I'm not doing your homework for you for a month. Maybe I'll never ever do it again."

"I forgot," Billy said, smiling. "That she was your friend, I mean. Doesn't matter, it'll grow. Teach her not to be so vain."

"How come you're the one to punish everyone for their faults? Who gave you the right to teach people lessons? Brute, beast, I hate you!"

Billy didn't seem to be listening. "If you don't do my homework," he said, after some thought. "I'll

148

clobber you so's you'll stay clobbered, know what I mean?" He winked at me.

"Clobber away, go ahead and see if I care, you bullying gasbag!" I shouted and ran ahead. I'd managed to become a bit fearless myself over the years, and at that moment I was so furious about Shirley's hair, I'd have taken on a whole army of Billys.

"Run away, go on!" he yelled after me. "Run away! GIRL! That's all you are, a silly girl. You only care about stupid Shirley's stupid old hair. You don't care about me."

It wasn't until much later, in bed, that I began to wonder if Billy was jealous of Shirley. I hadn't been playing with him nearly so much lately. It was very peculiar.

Anyway, one day we went on a class outing to the Castle, a kind of history outing it was supposed to be. We went in a coach with Miss Peters (we call her Miss Piggy because she's plump and pink, with yellow hair bouncing round her shoulders, and a really turned-up nose) and Mr Melville, who's dry and long like a stick with hair on top, and glasses. We took packed lunches from school and ate them in a field on the way. Most people were quite glad to be out for the afternoon, it didn't really matter what the reason was, but there were a few moaners, who kept saying things like:

"Boring old pile of rubbish."

"Should've skyved off."

"Why can't they leave us here to play football and collect us on the way back?"

"Are there dungeons? I vote we lock Miss Piggy in with Old Melville!"

"I wouldn't mind so much, only they'll probably get us to write about it tomorrow. Do a project even."

We drove along a bit more after lunch, and when we first saw the Castle through the windows of the

149

coach, everybody stopped talking. It was a very castle-like castle, square and high on top of a hill with tall, silent walls of thick, dark stone. I think Shirley was expecting a dainty turreted thing, like the Walt Disney cartoon castle in "Cinderella" or "The Sleeping Beauty."

"Gosh," she said to Miss Piggy, "it's so square and grim-looking."

Miss Piggy smiled: "Well, dear, it *is* used as a prison still, you know."

"Will we see them?" Shirley was anxious. "The prisoners, I mean?"

"No, of course not. We shall be going on the guided tour, and they're in quite another part of the buildings."

"We might hear their screams," said Billy, and shrieked with laughter.

"William Harrison, behave yourself," said Old Melville "or the screams you hear will be your own."

"What'll you do, sir, lock him in the dungeons?"

"Chain him to the wall?"

"Hang, draw and quarter him?"

"Stick his head on a spike on the castle walls?"

"SHUT UP!" I shouted, standing up in my seat. "Don't be disgusting!" I sat down again next to Shirley.

"I think boys are revolting sometimes," I said.

"It's not just the boys," said Shirley. "Lynn was the one who suggested chaining him to the wall."

"Then girls are revolting, too. Everyone's horrible to Billy."

"Billy's pretty horrible to them, though, isn't he?"

"Yes, I know. He is. Don't let's spoil the day by talking about him. I'm looking forward to it."

"I'm not, really," Shirley sighed. "All these old things, they just don't seem real to me. I can't sort of take them seriously, know what I mean? It's as if it

150

was a made-up story or something. I can't get worked up about things that happened donkey's years ago, not like you."

I kept quiet. I didn't admit to very many people that I found things that had happened long ago more real than a lot of the stuff that went on every day. I'd never told anyone, not even Shirley, that I couldn't go into St Peter's Square any more without reliving the Peterloo Massacre: seeing those soldiers charging about among the terrified crowds, mothers snatching children up from under the flying hooves, men running, falling, screaming, dying. Once, we went to visit a cotton mill, I had to leave the room, pretend I was feeling sick, because I could imagine so clearly the children, no older than me, sitting near the endlessly turning machines, deafened by long hours of that horrifying noise. It's not that I'm psychic or anything like that. I don't actually, physically *see* these things. It's just that I imagine them very strongly. After what happened to Billy, I asked myself over and over again whether I hadn't imagined the whole thing, but that was only to try and comfort myself, to convince myself that everything was in my own mind and nowhere else. But that's nonsense. It happened to everyone. To Billy most of all, of course, but something, something strange and something that I can't explain, happened to us all, even Miss Piggy and Old Melville.

When we got out of the coach, we went up some stone steps and waited for a while outside a small, wooden door that looked as if it hadn't been opened for centuries. But it did open, quite silently on well-oiled hinges and we went in.

The first room we saw was a courtroom, large and almost round, with high, light ceilings and a lot of heraldic shields up on the wall. The guide turned on a little silver tape-recorder and a voice spoke into the

151

silence of all of us sitting there, listening. The voice, floating up into the carvings over the windows, told us where to go next, and we followed the real guide into a small, round high room with tall walls, like a tower. Another tape-recorder (same voice) told us all about the things we could see all round us. Lots of people perked up a bit in this room, because it was full of horrible things in glass cases, like whips and cat-o-nine-tails (or cats-o-nine-tails, do you say?) and an iron, traplike contraption called a scold's bridle, which was put over women's heads and was supposed to stop them talking too much.

"My mum could do with that," someone said.

"What are those, sir, those kind of chains on the walls?" (These were prettily hung around like black Christmas paper chains.)

"Neck chains," said Mr Melville, "those big ones. And foot chains. Used to shackle people together on their way to the ships, to be deported to Australia."

Near the wall was a large wooden chair, Billy stood staring at it.

"What are you looking at that so carefully for?" I said.

"I'm trying to see how it works. It's jolly clever. You strap someone in, you see, and the more they struggle, the tighter the straps get. They used it for lunatics."

"Charming, I'm sure," I said and tried to laugh but the laughter wouldn't come. Everybody had turned quite quiet, even though the place was the opposite of gloomy. It should have been spooky, and it wasn't. It was neat, and brightly lit and quite cheerful in a peculiar kind of way. Even the dungeons, with thick stone walls and no light at all when the wooden doors were closed, were not too bad. We all took turns having the guide shut is in for a moment, and it wasn't very creepy, not with four or five others giggling and joking beside you, Miss Piggy came in with us, and Mr Melville went with the boys. Billy looked rather pale when he came out. He wasn't talking at all.

"I think it's a bit dull," Shirley said.

"No, it must have been awful," I replied, trying to picture it in detail and failing, miserably. "Think of that dark and the cold all the time, for months or years!"

"I know," said Shirley. "I know it was awful. But I can't *feel* it." I said nothing because I couldn't really feel it either, and I was worried to think that my imagination was losing its power. It was like losing your sight, in a funny kind of way.

The next room we went into was also a courtroom, and the tape-recorded voice spoke hollowly of the trials that had taken place there. A kind of double metal bracelet was fixed to the wall of the prisoner's dock, and in the olden days, people found guilty had their hands locked into the iron hands and the letter "M" for "Malefactor" branded on the fleshy part of their hand below the thumb. The branding-iron was still there, too. I didn't stay to look at it more carefully. Suddenly, I wanted to leave, quickly. Just for a split second, I thought I had seen him: the Judge. Dressed in purple or red, or black. I couldn't quite see, and he was gone almost before my imagination had pictured him there, thin, skeleton-like under the carved oak canopy above him, with eyes that could burn you deep inside more thoroughly than that hideous branding-iron in the dock. My imagination had come back with a vengeance, I thought as I hurried out. But Shirley had seen him, too. She was white.

"Did you see him?"

"Who?" (I was playing for time.)

"A man. Thin and white-faced, like a skull. He was only there for a second. Then he was gone."

"You must have imagined it." (I wasn't ready to admit anything at that stage.)

Shirley cheered up. "I'm sure I saw that man, but he can't have been real, can he, or he would have stayed put. Real people don't just vanish, do they?"

"No, of course they don't. Come on."

Shirley came, looking quite comforted. I couldn't think why. Surely she would rather have seen a real person who stayed put? Hadn't she worked out yet that if what she saw wasn't real, it could have been something else?

The room we went into (the last room we saw, as things turned out) is just a blur in my memory. I can't remember a word of the tape recording, nothing about the room at all except—well. As soon as we were all crowded in, a shaft of sunlight came straight through the narrow window, and all of a sudden it was as if that beam of brightness was the only thing in the world. I looked at it, feeling as if I was drowning in the light. While this was happening, I could feel without knowing why, that everyone else was drawn into the light, too, staring, staring and powerless to move. I vaguely remember Miss Piggy's mouth hanging open. The light faded a little, and then came the noise, so much noise that I covered my ears. There was mist now outside the window, mist everywhere, although the sun was still shining. I'm sure of that. Through the mist, I saw them. We all saw them. We talked about it afterwards. There were thousands and thousands of them: faces, people, screaming throats and waving arms, all over the castle walls. It was hard to see what they were wearing, but it wasn't modern clothes. The people were watching for something, waiting for something. I knew I didn't want to see what it was they were

154

waiting for. I took a deep breath and made a huge effort and turned my eyes away from the window. I saw Old Melville trembling, and blinking under his thick glasses. His mouth was opening and closing and his face was getting redder and redder. It was as if he were trying to speak and nothing would come.

"Are you all right, Mr Melville?" I said, because I honestly thought he was about to have a heart attack or something, and then two things happened.

Mr Melville shrieked out: "For God's sake, close your eyes, oh, close them, close them now. Don't look at it! Don't look at that hideous, that hideous ... gibbet. Oh, save these children, save them from seeing it!" He fell on his knees, crying like a first-former. Miss Piggy rushed towards him, and everyone turned to see what the commotion was about. I glanced at the window. Nothing. No people. Silence. No gallows. I was just breathing a sigh of relief when I heard Billy. Hadn't he been with us all the time?

"Kim! Kim! KIM!" The scream went right through me, into my bones. I felt so cold. I didn't know how I would move. But I ran. Faster than I've ever run before, shouting:

"Billy, Billy, I'm coming!" I could hear foot-steps behind me, and Miss Piggy calling. "Wait, Kim, wait for me!"

Billy was crouched on the floor of the courtroom, clutching his hand between his knees.

"My hand!" he moaned. "Oh, Kim, look at my hand. I can't stand it, the pain, how will I ever stand it?" He was crying and crying and rolling around to try and find a way to sit that wouldn't hurt so much.

"Let me see," I said. "Come on, Billy, let me see it."

"No, no," he sobbed, "nobody must see it. Please Kim, don't look!"

"Don't be such an idiot," I said. "How can we get it better if I don't see it?"

155

I reached down and took Billy's hand. Under the thumb, on the fleshy part of his left hand, clear as clear, the letter "M" was branded into the flesh: red, sore, burning. I dropped his hand in terror and turned to run away and find help. I bumped straight into Miss Piggy.

"Billy's hand is branded!" I shrieked. "It is! It is!"

"Shush, child, quiet. Sit down. Let me look at it." She sat down on a bench, and put her coat round me and went to look at Billy.

"He's fainted," she said. Mr Melville and the others had pushed their way into the room.

"Fetch an ambulance," said Miss Piggy.

"He's been branded," I cried. "Look at his hand."

"It's hurt, certainly" said Miss Piggy. "An ugly bruise and a bad cut, that's all, but it must be very painful. I wonder how he did that?"

"It's *not* a bruise," I shouted. "It's a mark. There's the branding iron. Touch it. Go on. Touch it."

I wouldn't touch it. I wouldn't look at the Judge's chair. I knew he would be there, the Judge. Miss Piggy and I went in the ambulance with Billy. Mr Melville took the others back to school.

Billy's hand has a scar on it now. Just a coincidence, I suppose, that the scar happens to have the shape of an "M"? That's the official story. They also said, the teachers and doctors, that the scar would fade. But it hasn't. Sometimes it's very pale and you can hardly see it, but sometimes it's very red and nasty. Billy rather enjoyed showing it off at first, but he never, not even to me, said a word about how he came to bear the mark in the first place.

The Dreamer of Dreams

Great-aunt Jonquil's timing was superb. She died in the middle of term, and her funeral was arranged for the morning of the Maths exam. Because my parents were abroad, I had to attend and represent our branch of the family. No gift that I could think of could possibly be as delightful as two days away from boarding-school at the start of Mock O-levels.

"But Frances, dear," said Miss Gosling, of the mauve angora bosom and forward-thrusting teeth, "you will have to attempt the papers you miss when you return. When you have recovered from your bereavement."

"Yes, Miss Gosling," I replied, looking as bereaved as possible. But I thought to myself that between today and Thursday anything could happen. Great-aunt Jonquil may have left me a million pounds on condition that I leave school at once. Even my grandmother would not insist on me coming back if *that* happened. There might be a fire while I was away, and I would return to find Miss Gosling picking with desolate fingers through the small heap of ashes that had been our papers. Anything could happen.

My friends were very excited. No one had ever been to a funeral before, and since Great-aunt Jonquil had not been a very close relative, we could all enjoy the thought of the occasion without feeling too sorry about the deceased. Angie lent me her best lipstick, called "Pink Adventure", Penny said I could take her new black gloves, and Kaye set my hair on rollers after supper. I went to sleep with my head in a spiked and torturing helmet, suffering (as Kaye put it) in order to be beautiful.

The next morning, a taxi came to take me to the station. As soon as I was on the train, I found a corner seat. Then I took off my school hat, and pushed the foul thing to the very bottom of my handbag, to crumple among the faded bits of pink and blue Kleenex. My school tie followed the hat into the messy abyss, then I took out the lipstick and put some on. It tasted of strawberries, so I licked it off, and put a little more on. I fluffed the curls out all over my head, and considered the effect in two inches of powdery mirror, which was the best I could manage. The hair wasn't bad, but the suffering had been in vain—I still wasn't beautiful. I looked out at the dead February landscape, the empty dripping branches of trees and the colourless sky, and felt extremely cheerful.

For a while, I ticked off in my mind the lessons I was missing. Gym and Geography and Double Maths went by, and the rain flew horizontally across the window. At half-past twelve, I took out my packed lunch. Miss Page, the school cook, had very little imagination. I knew, before I opened it, that there would be a stale buttered roll, a hard-boiled egg still in its shell, a bruised apple, a punch-drunk tomato, a wizened banana and a triangle of cheese. Last summer term, on a picnic at Pevensey Beach, Kay had said, "This isn't cheese—it's an intelligence test!" and indeed it was almost impossible to break into that silver skin. After lunch, I had a cigarette. I felt very daring and wicked, and half expected the lady sitting opposite to stop me, but she only smiled tenderly at her magazine, and wriggled her fat feet out of tight brown shoes. I stared at the other passengers for a while. No one looked remotely like a spy, or a drug-smuggler, or even a football hooligan, so I took out my book and tried to read. Perhaps it was not a very good book, or maybe I was too excited, but anyway, the print would not stay still. I put the book away, and, instead, began to think about Great-aunt Jonquil.

Rose, my grandmother, was the eldest of three sisters. Jonquil was the youngest. The middle one was called Lavender. Floral names are a tradition in my family. My mother is Iris, and my two aunts are Petunia and Violet. My father put his foot down when I was born, so that I have escaped the worst. My grandmother, however, like one of the malevolent fairies at the birth of the Sleeping Beauty, managed to slip a quick "Marigold" past my unsuspecting parents while I was being christened. We all refuse to admit it's there, and no one at school has even guessed that I have a second name at all.

Great-aunt Jonquil was a mystery. She lived far away across the other side of the country. She had, in her youth, married a Frenchman called La Valle, and had lived in Paris for many years. They came back to England just before the War, and apart from family weddings and christenings, we never saw her. I asked Granny Rose once if she missed her little sister.

"Not really, dear," was the reply. "She's a very busy lady, and always was a trifle strange."

"I'm sure I should love my sister dearly, if I had one," I said, a little shocked by such coolness.

"Oh, I *love* her, certainly," said Granny Rose. "Love is neither here nor there. We never had anything much to say to one another, that's all. It's even worse now. Poor Jonquil has become so foreign, especially since the death of herhusband."

That was true. It was one of the reasons I admired what little I knew of Great-aunt Jonquil. It was at my cousin Primrose's wedding that I last saw her. She arrived late, and waddled down the aisle, past the rows of lacy, pastel ladies, and grey and black men; past the tulle and the voile and the silk; past the gloves and top-hats and the knife-edge creases, like a scarlet Spanish treasure galleon let loose in Henley during the Regatta. From her wrists to her elbows she jingled gold bracelets. Her long dress was plum-coloured brocade, with a pattern of dragons, and on her head she wore something that made the other hats present look like left-over meringues. I suppose it must have been a hat. I was only nine at the time, and a bridesmaid with a great deal to think about, but I remember a knot of intertwining golden dragons with enormous green jewels for eyes. Scarlet ostrich feathers burned like fire out of their mouths and fell on either side of Great-aunt Jonquil's face, and their skin was iridescent, coruscating, almost alive.

Wisps of rude remarks blew around with the cigarette smoke during the reception: ". . . and original . . . an eccentric . . . in trade, my dear . . . Paris, what can you expect . . . fortunately no children . . . too much . . . an exhibition of herself . . ." I asked my father on the way home what he thought of Great-aunt Jonquil, and I remember his answer: "I admire the old bird," he said. "She has the courage to live her dreams, and the imagination to make others live theirs." I didn't understand exactly what he meant, and anyway, I fell asleep in the car, and forgot to ask him again when the excitement of the wedding was over.

The train finally arrived at my station. Aunt Petunia met me at the barrier, and we drove almost in silence towards Great-aunt Jonquil's house. I looked out of the windows, through the early dusk, at the rain-shiny streets of the dull little town. Aunt Petunia was driving with a surprised, vague look on her face, as if she did not know quite what to expect from a car. Every gear change successfully accomplished produced a grunt of pleasure. I think she thought of the car as some kind of mechanized horse. She was a horsey person. She said, "This car only needs a firm hand, you know. Needs to know who's master round here. She's not a bad old heap, by and large." Aunt Petunia always spoke like that. Every other phrase was a "by and large", or a "be that as it may", or a "far be it from me". Oscar, her husband, (". . . busy dealing with the legal side of things, dear"), was just like her. So were the children. I was glad they had measles and could not come to the funeral. We stopped at a red light. Aunt Petunia said suddenly, "Look, Franny, there's Aunt Jonquil's shop." It seemed very ordinary to me, although no one had ever told me that she kept a shop. I saw a small bow-fronted window, and a sign that said *LA VALLE MILLINERY SHOP*. In the window I could see a few hats: a puce felt one, and a flowery one, the kind of hat that everyone in the world wears, the kind of hat that screams out to be ignored. I couldn't believe it. Did the fascinating dragon-covered lady of my memories really sell hats like these? All the time? Then, just before the car leapt forward again, ("Steady as you go, old girl!" said Aunt Petunia), I saw it. There was a small notice pasted up to one of the panes of the window. It said *Your Dreams CAN Come True. Consult Mme La Valle Personally. Free Estimates Given*.

When we reached the house, my Aunt Violet bounced towards us with her usual cry of: "How divine to see you, darlings. I've just this minute put the kettle on. You must be parched." Her husband, Malcolm grunted a welcome at me and disappeared. Primrose, my married cousin, and her weedy hus-

161

band were there, too, but they were so absorbed with a slobbering squawking baby that they scarcely noticed me.

"Motherhood," said Aunt Violet later, from behind the teapot, "suits Primmy. It's made a woman of her." I personally thought she faded into the wallpaper rather more than usual, but I didn't say so.

Nobody did anything useful. Uncle Malcolm pottered, Uncle Oscar shuffled bits of paper around. More tea was made, poured and drunk. The baby had been fed, and burped and admired and put to bed. Then the others watched television, and I went exploring.

The house gave nothing away. It was boring. There was nothing in it that could not have belonged in a million other houses. I peered into the brown front room (side-board and upright piano), the dining-room (square mahogany table and tall chairs), the back room (television and green three-piece suite), and the morning room (assorted chairs, and cupboards full of ugly cups and saucers). Upstairs there were bedrooms with candlewick bedspreads and kidney-shaped dressing-tables, and net curtains. The baby was in the study, together with a lot of dark books and a small desk. I tried the door of the front bedroom last of all. It was locked, and I knew at once that *this*, this was the important room. This was where Great-aunt Jonquil had *lived*. Everything that had meant anything to her was in this room, I was sure of it. The rest of the house was as impersonal as an hotel.

After supper, Granny Rose and Great-aunt Lavender arrived. "There are things to be sorted through when a person dies," said Granny Rose, seeing how disorganized we were. She added, "It's no good being sentimental about it, Lavender."

"I'm sorry, Rose," said Great-aunt Lavender, wiping away a tear with the back of her hand, like a

162

small child. "Death is not only sad, it's also mortifying. To think of us picking over her things, her clothes, as if she had never been . . ."

"I've just this minute put the kettle on, Aunt Lavender," said Aunt Violet. "I'll put a little brandy in your tea, dear, shall I?"

"Please," sighed Great-aunt Lavender. I went up to her and whispered, "I know how you feel, Granty." The name was my shortened form of Great-aunt, which together with Lavender, was a little much. "You must miss her."

"Yes, I do. It was I, you see, who always had to look after her."

"Granty, do you know where the key is to the front bedroom?" I told her all about it.

We found the key in the end. Granny Rose had Jonquil's key-ring, and I simply asked to borrow it.

"May I come with you to unlock the room?" asked Granty.

"I'd love you to," I said. So we left the others counting cups and saucers, knives and forks, napkins and tablecloths, making an inventory of all the furniture, and cutting sandwiches and icing cakes for what Granny Rose called a "collation" after tomorrow's funeral. We walked upstairs together, and I found the key quite quickly and opened the door.

"Turn the light on, dear," said Granty. "I think it's a little to your left."

"Yes, I've got it . . ." I began, and could not continue Granty stood silently beside me, and we both stared. Think of everything beautiful in the world: think of flowers, pearls, fruit, soft feathers; think of velvet and satin and silver and gold; think of lace and sequins and yards of silk; think of rainbow taffeta and clouds of net; think of gems and crowns and fans and veils—it was all there in that room, heaped onto

163

a long table, spilling from a cupboard, piled onto the bed.

"This was Jonquil's workroom," said Granty. "This was where she made them."

"The hats for the shop, do you mean?"

"No, dear, not those. She bought those wholesale, I think. No, this room was for the Others."

"What Others?" I asked.

Granty sat down suddenly on the end of the bed. "They don't like to talk about it." She pointed downstairs. "Rose thinks it's childish, and Petunia and Violet have never shown the least interest. Your mother, now, was an imaginative child, but ..." Granty paused and smiled and looked at me. "It's a funny thing."

"What is?"

"That Rose should have had three children, and that Jonquil and I should have had none. Now I'm not saying anything against Rose, you understand ..."

"No, of course you aren't. I *do* understand," I said.

"... but she has never learnt to dream. Or perhaps she has forgotten. It was partly the fault of our mother, of course."

I settled myself happily on the floor for a long chat.

"Rose was the eldest, and Mama was quite useless. I think she was probably a clever woman, you know, and part of her cleverness was her ability to make other people work for her. Rose did the organizing for the family from the day that Father died. She was eight then, and I was five. Jonquil was a baby. It is, therefore, hardly surprising that Rose never had time to dream."

"And you looked after Jonquil?"

"Yes, I did. And later, when we grew up a little, Jonquil and I ..." Granty stopped and wiped her eyes.

164

"Would you like to borrow my hanky?" I asked.

"Yes, please, dear. I am silly, but I remember it so clearly."

"It *is* fun to hear all these things," I said. "Do go on."

"Yes, well, Jonquil and I had a game. I must have been about twelve, I suppose, and Jonquil was eight. It was the kind of game every child plays: 'What would you like to be when you grow up?' A sort of acting game. But there were two important things about it, you see, and both were Jonquil's idea. First, you could never choose to be anything ordinary, like a nurse or a teacher. What was *possible* was ruled out, entirely. It was really a game of 'What would you like to be in your wildest dreams?' Things like queens, bareback-riders in a circus, and fortune-tellers were allowed, and of course every kind of fairy and monster. The second thing about the game was that Jonquil used everything she could lay her hands on to make these dreams come true. As true as she could make them. All Mama's jewels and scarves and feather boas, all Rose's long dresses and ribbons were turned into costumes of barbaric splendour, and even at that age, Jonquil could decorate a straw boater so that it looked like the headdress of the Empress of China." Granty grinned suddenly. "We paid for our pleasure, of course. Mama was too vague to worry about what went on in her cupboards, but Rose . . . she hated us meddling with her things. Once she locked us in this very room for hours with nothing to eat. We quite enjoyed it. We played prisoners, and had great fun groaning and starving to death."

"Was that when Great-aunt Jonquil started being interested in hats?"

"Yes, that was the beginning." Granty stood up, and went over to the window. "Jonquil and I went to Paris together in the spring of 1927. I was considered a suitable chaperone at the age of 22, which tells you a lot about what an awkward, plain-looking, dull creature I was."

"You're *not* plain," I said quickly. "You're very elegant and distinguished."

Granty laughed. "Maybe I've grown old gracefully. But you should have seen me in 1927. As I've said: the perfect chaperone. Jonquil, now, was beautiful. She was better than beautiful, she was alive. Every bit of her was alive, and just to look at her made other people feel happy. I can't explain it properly, I'm afraid."

"But I know exactly what you mean," I said.

"Yes, maybe you do . . . Anyway, as it turned out, I was not such a very good chaperone. Jonquil was a strongwilled girl and we always seemed to be doing exactly what she wanted. We met the most exciting people: painters, and poets and musicians. We sat in cafés, and walked in the markets, and along the Seine. Paris is a magic city. And then one day, I fell in love. Jonquil told me later that she had stage-managed it all, winking and dropping gloves around a young man who lived in our *pension*. One day he picked up a glove and introduced himself. Jonquil remembered a pressing appointment which did not exist, and that was that. I was in love. Two weeks later, we were engaged. Like a fool, I took the young man to England to meet Mama and Rose. Jonquil thought I was mad, and she was right. I should have married him on the spot. I see that now. Instead, I took him home, where Rose disapproved, and showed it, and Mama had the vapours and talked of 'marrying beneath you' and disgrace, until I was in such a muddle that I simply broke off the engagement for the sake of peace." Granty blew her nose into the hanky. "I'm such a weak character."

"I would never give up the man I loved," I said firmly.

"That's right, dear. You're quite right. But people put pressure on, you see, and not everyone can stand it. Jonquil never forgave Rose for that." Granty giggled. "I'm sure at least *one* of the reasons why she married La Valle was because he was a lion-tamer in the Cirque Médrano."

"A lion-tamer? *Really*?" I couldn't believe it.

"Yes," said Granty, "and a very gentle charming man, too. But you can imagine how Mama and Rose reacted when they heard! I returned to England and the young couple took a small studio in the Rue du Texel. Jonquil began making and selling hats. La Valle continued to tame his lions. Jonquil and I wrote to one another regularly. Then in 1937, a lion savaged poor La Valle and they both came to England, to this town. Jonquil bought the shop, and began to sell hats here. She noticed the kind of hat that people wore, and in order to make money quickly (for she was the only breadwinner) she stocked models for which there was a demand. La Valle died just after the beginning of the war, and Jonquil went to work in a factory. People didn't think about hats for seven years.

"When the war was over, the shop was reopened. I used to visit Jonquil quite often in those days, and one evening, sitting in this very room, she reminded me of our childhood game. 'Wouldn't it be fun, Lav,' she said, 'to turn these poor, austerity-clad, ration-book women into fairy princesses? To make their dreams come true?' I thought she was joking, but the very next day she pasted a notice to the window of her shop."

"Yes, I've seen it," I said. "*Your dreams can come true. Consult Mme La Valle Personally.*"

"That's the one. Well, they came. All the dream-starved women of this dream-starved town, and Jonquil turned them from the neck up into whatever they wanted to be. Ladies would save their clothing coupons for months and spend them at Jonquil's, having their fantasies tailor-made. I said to her once, 'Surely no one would dare to wear these miraculous hats about the streets, would they?' and she smiled and said, 'Well, they can dress up at home whenever they like, and besides, I give parties ...' Once a month the ladies would gather downstairs, and sip French coffee and admire one another. Maybe, for a short while, each one pretended to be someone she was not. I don't know. I think Jonquil thought of herself as a therapist. She used to say, 'If it makes them feel good, feel truly themselves, then that's enough.' She offered to make me a hat. She wanted me to tell her my dreams. But I refused. I could never wear it, living with Rose. Can you imagine what she would say?'

"Not really," I laughed.

"There you are, Franny darling: the story of our lives, just about. It's made me feel much better just to talk about it." Granty gave me back my hanky. "I suppose we ought to go down and help now, don't you think?"

She locked the door and went downstairs.

Sandwich-cutting was nearly over, the uncles had gone into the dining-room to talk about the will, and the sale of the shop. I began to wash up the dishes that had piled up in the sink, and Granty sat at the kitchen table looking useful.

"There's someone at the back door," said Aunt Petunia suddenly.

Granny Rose said, "Nonsense, dear, it's your imagination. I didn't hear anything."

We all listened. A soft scratching noise fell into the silence.

"Whoever can that be, at such a time?" said Granny Rose. She pulled the door open and a faded mouse-grey little woman almost fell into the kitchen.

"I'm so sorry to intrude at such a time," whispered this person. "I know how grief-stricken you must all be. But I just wondered . . . I'm a friend of Mme La Valle's and I just wondered if . . ."

The woman was not allowed to continue. Granny Rose pushed her into a chair, Petunia took her coat, and Violet presented her with a cup of tea.

"Now," said my Granny, "I'm afraid I didn't quite catch your name."

"Trebucket. Maud Trebucket. I only popped in to offer condolences, and to ask a great favour. You see, Mme La Valle had many friends here, and we would all consider it an honour if we were allowed to attend the funeral."

Maud Trebucket paused. I could see Granny Rose and my two aunts thinking of polite ways to say "No". But Granty spoke first, and very strongly:

"Certainly you must all come. Jonquil would have been very pleased, I'm sure. It's a kind thought and we're most grateful."

Granny Rose looked at Granty. I think she was sorry that she couldn't lock an old lady into a room with nothing to eat for hours on end. Maud Trebucket trembled with gratitude, finished her tea and left. The minute the back door closed behind her, everyone began to attack Granty. She didn't say a word.

Quite suddenly, they all made me angry."Oh, for heaven's sake," I yelled, "STOP IT! These ladies were Great-aunt Jonquil's *friends*, and I bet she'd rather have them at her funeral than a lot of bickering relations who didn't come near her when she was alive."

I was *not* an old woman. Granny Rose does not tolerate such behaviour from a child. I was ordered to my room, and told to get a good night's sleep. "It's all been too much for you, poor Franny," said Aunt Violet, soothingly. Her hand wavered over the teapot. I stopped myself from throwing a plate at her blue sausage-curled head, and left the room.

Next morning, we all sat stiff and quiet in our funeral clothes, waiting for the shiny cars to arrive. It was raining. Granny Rose, Petunia and Violet were in black from head to toe. I wore my navy blue school suit, with a black chiffon scarf tied around my neck. Primrose and her family were not going to the funeral. She said, "We'll see to things this end." There was nothing to see to. All the sandwiches, cakes and cold meats lay under neat damp muslin shrouds on the dining-room table. Granty came down late, looking beautiful in a pale blue suit and a high-necked lace blouse. Granny Rose sipped her coffee menacingly. "That outfit," she said to her sister, "would be more fitting at a wedding." I closed my eyes and prayed that Granty would stick up for herself. She did.

"Nonsense, Rose," she replied, calmly. "You know yourself that Jonquil detested black. She used to say that no one over thirty should be allowed to wear it. Since it is Jonquil's funeral, I am wearing colours she would have liked." That was that. I wished with all my heart that I had brought my party dress to wear. I did not want to be lumped together with Granny Rose, Petunia and Violet. I smiled and winked at Granty, and she smiled back.

The shiny cars arrived. Great-aunt Jonquil's yellowish coffin was in the first one. There were no flowers. I squeezed into the second car, next to Granty.

"Why are there no flowers?" I asked.

"Jonquil forbade it. Flowers are for the living, she said, not for the dead."

In the church, we all sat bunched together in the

170

front row. Candles flickered in the greenish daylight, and someone unseen was playing something gloomy on the organ. Granty whispered, "How Jonquil would have hated this! Especially that organ."

I began to imagine the kind of funeral Jonquil would have liked. Lots of bright colours and *La vie en rose* on the accordion? I had to stop myself from giggling. The music washed around us, an ocean of sound. We all looked solemn and waited with our hands in our laps. Uncle Malcolm couldn't stop coughing. Granny Rose raised an eyebrow at him.

Then I heard it, a clicking sound of many feet tiptoeing on the marble floor, like an army of mice in high-heeled shoes.

"Jonquil's friends, I suppose," whispered Granty, and was too well-bred to turn round. The others all sat with their faces set, as if they hadn't heard. I looked.

I saw about a dozen ladies, sitting in two neat rows on either side of the aisle. One of the ladies smiled and waved at me. I suppose it must have been Maud Trebucket, although I didn't recognize her.

"Granty," I muttered, "you *must* look. The dream-hats have come."

Just then, the vicar arrived and the service began. I couldn't wait for it to be over, couldn't wait to be outside, to get a really good look at the hats.

Later, in the church porch, we met the ladies. Maud Trebucket introduced them. She looked transformed. Her grey suit and black shoes were quite ordinary, but on her head she wore a festival of spring flowers and vines. Miniature doves peeped between the roses, and shimmering butterflies hovered about precariously on visible wires. Miss Trebucket was the embodiment of Spring. A Mrs Chaunce had a pagoda on her head, and golden bells tinkled as she walked her own private Road to Mandalay. Miss Wynkell, well-corseted in brown tweed, was adorned with gem-encrusted feathers. The Gathercole sisters wore Spanish mantillas over high, tortoiseshell combs. There were two gipsy ladies, all writhing ribbons and fringed scarves. There was a medieval princess, wearing a delicate, silver cornet, and another lady had wax fruit cunningly heaped among corn sheaves, towering above her thin face. I admired them. It must have taken a great deal of courage to walk through the streets of this town, where they were all well-known, dressed like that.

I said to Granty, "How do they dare?"

She answered: "Jonquil showed them. If they wanted to be goddesses of Spring, or Spanish ladies, then they had to show courage. A commitment to their dreams."

We left after a while. I looked out of the back window of the car as we drove away. The ladies became smaller and smaller, their fabulous head-dresses fading, vanishing at last in a blur of rain.

"I think," said Aunt Petunia, "that that went off very well, in the circumstances." She hung her black coat in the cloakroom and hurried with Aunt Violet to see whether Primrose had removed the muslin shrouds.

"Jonquil would have been pleased, I think, to see all her friends looking so fine," said Granty, patting her hair and looking into the spotty mirror which hung in the hall.

"You talk a lot of nonsense sometimes, Lavender, for a woman of your age," said Granny Rose. "It was a disgusting exhibition, a fancy-dress party, no less. I think that some respect should have been shown to *us*. Our wishes should have been considered a little. Jonquil, after all, is dead."

She turned and left us. Granty looked sad. I said, "Would you like to borrow my hanky again?"

172

"No, dear, thank you. I'm not sad. I'm just feeling rather sorry for Rose."

At that moment, the guests arrived. The bank manager, a sprinkling of neighbours, the vicar and his wife, the lawyer and his wife, all drank sherry and swallowed sandwiches and crumbled bits of cake all over the carpet. The vicar's wife very carefully picked the icing off her cake and popped it between purple lips, leaving on her plate small mountains and valleys of yellow sponge. The lawyer told jokes and the uncles dutifully snorted. One of the neighbours was trying tactfully to discover whether the house was being sold. Aunt Violet, at a loose end with no tea to make, was crawling around the floor, shaking her blue curls into the baby's face. He was not amused. Neither was Granny Rose. "Violet dear," she said, "do come and meet Mr Pickerel, the Bank Manager. He has been such a tremendous help." Aunt Violet obeyed, and the baby was left with his parents. Granty came over and spoke to me.

"Frances dear, there is something I want to tell you. Come into the hall for a moment." I followed her out of the room.

"What is it, Granty?"

"Jonquil left me some things in her will, you know. Among other things, the contents of her workroom. I have the keys here. I'd like you to go up and choose something for yourself. Something that will remind you . . . remind you of Jonquil, and remind you also never to forget how to dream. Maybe something that will encourage you."

"Encourage me? Encourage me to do what?"

"I mean give you courage. To make your wildest dreams come true. Courage not to give up what you really want to do. Courage to be yourself."

She held out the key ring and I took it and went upstairs.

After a long time. I chose a fan. It was tiny, no bigger than my hand when it was spread out. The sticks were ivory, carved in a pattern of leaves and flowers, and the silk that covered the sticks was as thin as woven light. Painted on the silks in delicate colours was a picture of a girl in a red dress, standing in a garden full of blossom and silver-blue birds. I found soft tissue paper in one of the cupboards, and gently, gently, wrapped my fan in it. Then I locked the room up, and went downstairs to show Granty what I had chosen.

The next day, I travelled back to school, thinking of the Maths exam. My packed lunch this time was leftovers from yesterday: ham sandwiches, and egg sandwiches, and hard bits of cake with some of the icing chipped off. The vicar's wife had probably had a go at them. The sun was shining, and I felt miserable. As the train drew into the station, I rescued my school hat from the bottom of my bag, and brushed the dust from it with my crumpled tie. I put the tie on, and rubbed my lipstick off. I didn't bother to look in the mirror—I knew exactly what I looked like.

In the taxi driving up to school, I began to cheer up a little. I thought of the fan. I thought of telling my friends. Wait till they heard about the ladies in the church, about my Great-uncle, the French lion-tamer; about Great-aunt Jonquil's bedroom.

Miss Gosling met me in the Front Hall. "Well, Frances," she said, "back in our midst, I see."

What answer could I possibly give? I was miles away, worlds away.

"Yes, thank you, Miss Gosling," I said. Then I went to look for my friends.

General Editors: Anne and Ian Serraillier

Chinua Achebe Things Fall Apart
Douglas Adams The Hitchhiker's Guide to the Galaxy
Vivien Alcock The Cuckoo Sister; The Monster Garden; The Trial of Anna Cotman
Michael Anthony Green Days by the River
Bernard Ashley High Pavement Blues; Running Scared
J G Ballard Empire of the Sun
Stan Barstow Joby
Nina Bawden The Witch's Daughter; A Handful of Thieves; Carrie's War; The Robbers; Devil by the Sea; Kept in the Dark; The Finding; Keeping Henry
Judy Blume It's Not the End of the World; Tiger Eyes
E R Braithwaite To Sir, With Love
John Branfield The Day I Shot My Dad
F Hodgson Burnett The Secret Garden
Ray Bradbury The Golden Apples of the Sun; The Illustrated Man
Betsy Byars The Midnight Fox
Victor Canning The Runaways; Flight of the Grey Goose
John Christopher The Guardians; Empty World
Gary Crew The Inner Circle
Jane Leslie Conly Racso and the Rats of NIMH
Roald Dahl Danny, The Champion of the World; The Wonderful Story of Henry Sugar; George's Marvellous Medicine; The BFG; The Witches; Boy; Going Solo; Charlie and the Chocolate Factory; Matilda
Andrew Davies Conrad's War
Anita Desai The Village by the Sea
Peter Dickinson The Gift; Annerton Pit; Healer
Berlie Doherty Granny was a Buffer Girl
Gerald Durrell My Family and Other Animals
J M Falkner Moonfleet
Anne Fine The Granny Project
F Scott Fitzgerald The Great Gatsby
Anne Frank The Diary of Anne Frank

Leon Garfield Six Apprentices
Graham Greene The Third Man and The Fallen Idol; Brighton Rock
Marilyn Halvorson Cowboys Don't Cry
Thomas Hardy The Withered Arm and Other Wessex Tales
Rosemary Harris Zed
Rex Harley Troublemaker
L P Hartley The Go-Between
Esther Hautzig The Endless Steppe
Ernest Hemingway The Old Man and the Sea; A Farewell to Arms
Nat Hentoff Does this School have Capital Punishment?
Nigel Hinton Getting Free; Buddy; Buddy's Song
Minfong Ho Rice Without Rain
Anne Holm I Am David
Janni Howker Badger on the Barge; Isaac Campion
Kristin Hunter Soul Brothers and Sister Lou
Barbara Ireson (Editor) In a Class of Their Own
Jennifer Johnston Shadows on Our Skin
Toeckey Jones Go Well, Stay Well
James Joyce A Portrait of the Artist as a Young Man
Geraldine Kaye Comfort Herself; A Breath of Fresh Air
Clive King Me and My Million
Dick King-Smith The Sheep-Pig
Daniel Keyes Flowers for Algernon
Elizabeth Laird Red Sky in the Morning
D H Lawrence The Fox and The Virgin and the Gypsy; Selected Tales
Harper Lee To Kill a Mockingbird
Laurie Lee As I Walked Out One Midsummer Morning
Julius Lester Basketball Game
Ursula Le Guin A Wizard of Earthsea
C Day Lewis The Otterbury Incident
David Line Run for Your Life; Screaming High
Joan Lingard Across the Barricades; Into Exile; The Clearance; The File on Fraulein Berg
Penelope Lively The Ghost of Thomas Kempe
Jack London The Call of the Wild; White Fang
Lois Lowry The Road Ahead; The Woods at the End of Autumn Street

How many have you read?